It Happens Between Stops

A collection of writings

By

CIE WORKERS

Edited by Mattie Lennon

ORIGINAL WRITING.

© 2010 VARIOUS
Cover design by Zeff Lawless
zeff@graffitidesign.ie
Title by John Bolton

978-1-907179-89-1

A CIP catalogue for this book is available from the National Library.

Published by ORIGINAL WRITING LTD., Dublin, 2010.

Printed by CAHILL PRINTERS LIMITED, Dublin.

INTRODUCTION

by Lawrence Block

Past incarnations aside, I first got to Ireland in 1964. My then wife and I flew to Shannon and drove down through Conor Pass to Dingle, arriving just in time to watch the Rose of Tralee alight from her boat. ("But Mummy," a child piped up, "it's just a girl. I thought it was going to be a real rose.")

My next visit was in early 1967. I came alone this time, spent a month in Dublin finishing a novel, then drifted south and west to Bantry, in West Cork. That's where I first heard of Listowel. I was staying at a hotel called the Anchor, and in the bar one night a fellow was talking about a playwright named John B. Keane, who kept a pub in Listowel, and what a place it was for good conversation. "Sometimes," he said, "the stories just roll."

I thought about having a look at Listowel, but went home instead. A couple of years later---the summer of 1971, it must have been---I was back, with my wife and daughters along. We spent a month or more, and wound up in Listowel, where we stayed at Mount Rivers and spent evenings at John B's and heard all about Listowel Writers Week. "You'll have to come next year," everyone said.

I met Sean McCarthy at John B's, and we took to each other at once. My wife and I did in fact come back to Listowel the following spring, and the year after that, participating in Writers Week and logging long hours at John B's. And then in the summer of 1973 our marriage ended. I did get to Writers Week on my own in 1974, but it felt strange to be there, and I was drunk most of the time, and went home feeling out of sorts.

Two years later I ran into Sean again, but not in Listowel. I met him in Greenville, South Carolina, where his wife Carol owned a nursing home. (They met on a plane, where they discovered that they each lived in Greenville, one in South Carolina, one in North Kerry.) I had given up my apartment in New

York and was heading south and west, intending to get to Los Angeles eventually. I stopped in Greenville where a friend of mine was working at an advertising agency, and he fixed me up on a date with a local divorcee, and it turned out we have a friend in common---Sean McCarthy, remarkably enough.

I moved on to Charleston, and the lady from Greenville visited me there, and a few months later I still hadn't reached Los Angeles, and returned to Greenville to spend Christmas with her and her friends, including Sean and Carol.

I remember one morning when Sean imparted a bit of wisdom gained over the course of a rich lifetime. "Beer's all right," he said, "but whiskey's a bad bastard."

What I learned for myself was that beer was a bad bastard, too, and so was anything with alcohol in it. By the spring of 1977 I'd had enough of it, and had the good fortune to stop. I found myself with a new life to live, and set about living it, and Listowel seemed unlikely to play a role therein.

Fast forward eighteen years. 1995, I think it was, and a publisher had me doing a book tour in the UK, and wanted to include a few days in Dublin. I'd remarried by then, to a woman who'd herself been to Ireland a time or two, and when the book tour ended we decided to treat ourselves to a week or so in Ireland. I'd talked a lot about Listowel, and that's where we headed.

We checked into the Arms and walked over to John B's. He'd gone to bed early, but Mary was behind the bar, and to my surprise she remembered me. I asked about this friend and that friend, and it began to seem as though everyone I'd known had died since my last visit. "Gone to Heaven," Mary said gently, time and time again.

One who'd gone was Sean. I'd thought of him so many times over the years, and always thought I'd see him again. But I'd left it too long.

We came back in the spring, Lynne and I, and took part in Writers Week. And after that we attended more years than not. In 1998 I flew over a month early; I had a book to write, and decided I'd hole up at the Arms and get it written. The very first afternoon I walked over to St. John's, where Joe Murphy sold me a ticket to a play that was to run that evening. There were only a handful of people in the audience, and I took a seat in the first row, as I'm apt to do. The play was a rather free adaptation of Lysistrata, and it began with the female lead appearing onstage stark naked. She then put on a garment and the play began.

When it ended I went over to John B's, where I hoisted my usual glass of mineral water. And the visiting players were there as well, and the conversation was fine as it always is in that establishment, and I found the actress to be good company even when she was wearing clothes. I went back to my hotel and went to bed, and in the morning I started my book, and had it finished in time for Writers Week.

It is a remarkable town, Listowel. It has changed a good deal in the forty years I've known it. The square, once a place where farmers parked their donkey carts, is one of the prettiest in the country. New houses---McMansions, some of them---circle the town on what once were country lanes. The pubs, astonishingly, are smoke-free.

And I'm sure it's continued to change in the five years since my last visit. I went once after John B's death, and for me his absence took the joy out of Writers Week.

I suppose I'll get back one of these years. Somewhere along the way they made me a Vice-President of the Festival, and that's the sort of wholly honorary position I'm pleased to hold, one that doesn't require that one actually do anything. Still, I ought to show up sooner or later, don't you think?

It was on my last visit, at an open Mic session, in John B's, that Mattie Lennon (having told a story that you couldn't repeat to your maiden aunt) *sold* me a copy of "There's Love And There's Sex And There's The 46A." It was a collection of stories, articles poems and essays by CIE workers.

And now, it's my great pleasure to introduce you to *It Happens Between Stops* this latest, splendid, selection of CIE literature. The quantity and quality of work produced by this group, taken from a workforce of a few thousand people, would do credit to a city of many millions. So it should not surprise you that there are good things to be found within this volume's covers.

For my part, I was especially taken with "And All His Songs Were Sad," which so beautifully brings into focus the life and work of my old friend Sean McCarthy.

Lawrence Block
New York City

SPONSORS

Dublin Bus

Bus Eireann

Irish Rail

CIE Credit Union

NBRU

SIPTU

TSSA

General Purposes, Donnybrook

General Purposes, Phibsborough

Corporate Catering

Powerscourt Estate

Avoca Handweavers

Shannon Heritage

Irish Traction Group

CONTENTS

THERE IS SOMETHING ABOUT MARY

Pat Cavanagh

You could not help noticing Mary. She was tall and tanned with long blonde hair and beautiful green eyes. She would crack her fingers in class one at a time - or all at once - if she was bored. When she laughed or smiled (which she did often) it was impossible to be cross with her, no matter how much this disrupted the class. She would ask permission to speak, and without waiting for a reply, would launch into an impassioned appeal to save the starving children in Africa, defend the environment, or shut down the nuclear reactor at Sellafield. By the time she was finished, maybe five minutes later, she would have the entire class spellbound. You could be sure no more class work would be done for the rest of the day as Mary and her class mates organised themselves for the coming campaign. There was very little I could do – I realised I had a truly remarkable personality in my class.

About three months ago, we were doing music. I had asked the children to bring along some of their favourite music. Mary's father had been a singer in a band when he was young. She had grown up in a house full of music, as he still played part time. While the others brought in the latest top ten hits, she brought in music by the Beatles, Rolling Stones, Mozart and Beethoven, as well as many other well-known singers and musicians from the 1960s and 1970s. She explained the subtleties and the wonders of a whole range of music from Abba to ZZ Top, using examples that she copied on to a CD. I know quite a lot about music from that period, but I have to admit I was awestruck by the depth and breadth of knowledge of a girl who was not even born when all this music was happening. I worried slightly as to what she had up her sleeve for her classmates.

She decided that the school needed a school band, and that her classmates were going to be the band members. Now, our school is in a very disadvantaged area of the city, so asking parents for funding was out of the question. Mary had thought of that, and within two minutes had started the class writing letters (she dictated, the class wrote) to a hundred local and national businesses seeking sponsorship. The letter was very clever. We would like your help in training our school band; do you have staff who would be willing to spare their time and energy to teach us how to play music; could you help us to acquire working second-hand guitars, drums, a keyboard and so on; we are not looking for cash. Each letter was written by hand. The letters were delivered by hand all over the city that evening by a small army of her classmates on their bikes.

The results were astonishing! Dozens of people, including many well-known faces in the music business wanted to become involved. Every Saturday morning the school hall rocked as the students practiced music and singing under the guidance of skilled and talented people who once were famous in their own times. Word spread, and one day they were invited to appear on national television.

Mary didn't tell anyone about the pain until she collapsed in class. The ambulance seemed to take ages to arrive. She forced her big smile for a paramedic who told her that his son had changed from local thug to guitar player extraordinaire thanks to her influence. Mary had just finished telling us about avoiding antisocial behaviour, but had not been her usual self while speaking. An hour later, during a break, I phoned the emergency department and was told she had had a cardiac arrest in the ambulance but had been resuscitated by the ambulance staff. A police car had collected her parents and they were with her. The outlook was not good.

I can't remember the rest of that day or the days that followed. Sure, class continued without interruptions and without periodic cracking of fingers. But things were very quiet until just before class broke up for a midterm break. The headmaster called me aside and told me that Mary had had another cardiac arrest and was not expected to survive. She was unconscious. When I told the class that Mary was very ill, they decided there and then they would sing and play for her. We all trooped down to the music hall, collected the instruments, and then marched to the hospital. The school band squeezed into the hospital's tiny chapel, and Mary, wired to various machines, was then wheeled in. She seemed to be asleep, but somehow she managed her big smile when the music started.

Now, I'm not a religious person, but I'll swear to my dying day a miracle happened that afternoon. Gradually the colour came back to her face. Her hands and then her feet moved with the music. She tried to sing along. Her parents didn't know whether to laugh or cry. Two days later, she was sitting up and chatting to everyone around. The doctor told her he would fix the bad blood vessel to her heart by sliding a tiny instrument up one of the veins in her leg under local anaesthetic. She could watch the x-ray if she wanted. Three weeks later, she was back in school, cracking her fingers, disrupting the class with impromptu speeches, and flashing her smiles. Yes, there is something about Mary.

Brutal or beautiful?

Mark Bolger

Boxing as a sport seems to have gotten a beating over recent years. Now I ask myself is this due to the fact that diet and training methods have improved drastically, leading to the idea that the fighters are getting more of a punishment during the bouts? Which in turn is leading to this public outcry to tighten up the rules to protect the contestants. Or is it that it has received such notoriety both good and bad that it has ended up in the attention view of compulsive critics. Now my first impulse would be to re-direct their attention to the obvious, and that would be that boxing is no more dangerous than most other sports. Footballers receive career ending injuries, race car drivers risk their lives every day in the pursuit of their sport, skiing, deep-sea diving ... etc. Every sport has had victims of so called freak accidents that could be called up as an argument to show the dangers of a sport, I've even heard of a tiddly-winks champion who lost an eye due to a rogue tiddly. Having listened to all this bad press I feel it is my place to show a little truth of the noble sport of pugilism. To begin this task I think a bit of history would be the best starting point.

Boxing or Pugilism has been recorded dating back as far as 4000BC in Egypt recently revealed in Hieroglyphic evidence. The spread of boxing followed the expansion of Egyptian civilization through the Mediterranean and the Middle East reaching ancient Greece by as early as 1500BC. By 686BC boxing had been refined and perfected enough to be included in the Olympic Games. However, the sport bore little resemblance to what is now known as boxing. Matches were held outdoors, with spectators forming the boundaries. The fight continued without pause until one participant was unable to continue. Evidence is also around to show boxing present throughout the ages right up to the Roman Empire, then with the rise of Christianity and the decline of the Roman Empire pugilism as entertainment apparently ceased to exist for some centuries.

Jack Broughton recognized by some as the father of boxing, is credited with taking the first steps leading to boxing's acceptance as a respectable athletic endeavour in today's 'civilised' society by introducing "mufflers," the forerunners of modern gloves, to protect one's hands and the opponent's face. Broughton devised the sport's first set of rules in 1743, and those rules, with only minor changes, governed boxing until they were replaced by the more detailed London Prize Ring rules in 1838.

Though the London Prize Ring rules did much to help boxing, the brawling that distinguished old-time pugilism continued to alienate most of England's upper class, and it became apparent that still more revisions were necessary to attract a better class of patron. John Graham Chambers of the Amateur Athletic Club devised a new set of rules in 1867, which emphasized boxing technique and skill. Chambers sought the patronage of John Sholto Douglas, the 9th Marquess of Queensberry, who lent his name to the new guidelines. The Queensberry rules differed from the London rules in four major respects: contestants wore padded gloves; a round consisted of three minutes of fighting followed by a minute of rest; wrestling was illegal, and any fighter who went down had to get up unaided within 10 seconds, if he could not do so, he was declared knocked out, and the fight was over.

Professionals, who considered them unmanly, first scorned the new rules and championship bouts continued to be fought under London Prize Ring rules. But many young pugilists preferred the Queensberry guidelines and this aided the rise, which led to their universal use today.

I personally think that one of the reasons for its apparent distaste is that by the early 20th century, boxing had become a shortcut to riches and social acceptance for those near the foot of the economic ladder. Now, even given it's noble upbringing and obvious place in the annals of history and sport it is still derided as a sport second only to hare coursing and fox hunting (which ironically is supported by the upper classes that seem to find boxing so objectionable). The people who should be boxing's champions (excuse the pun) are those intimately involved in the sport, not those who look on in distaste convincing themselves that by changing the sport their misplaced altruism is in fact helping prevent the injury of those in the ring.

As a former boxer I feel it is my place to don the mantle and try to show what makes a boxer want to box. The history of boxing speaks for itself and its popularity throughout the ages cannot be reasoned by something as simple as men wanting to hit each other. It's true that the main entrants to the sport are those who may not have a lot, come from bad neighbourhoods or poor backgrounds, but these people are the ones who hold the need to succeed and see that success in the physical arena is more achievable to them than academia or the business world, simply because of the lack of opportunity their social standing allows them. The attraction to the sport first begins with a young boy needing some outlet to establish his identity. A young boy saying 'I'm a boxer' and probably for the first time in his life give himself a label which proves to him that he is not just a statistic and is actually somebody of worth, it also gives him an outlet for the frustration of working class life. These reasons supersede the fear of getting hit, which is what separates those that will from those that won't. Then as training progresses and the realisation that there is more to this sport than just trying to hit and avoid being hit by your opponent. The knowledge of your coach becomes more and more impressive to you as he lays down yet another philosophy on why you should bob then instead of weaving, or follow through when your preservation instincts are telling you to go on the defensive. The day finally comes when you recognize during yet another sparring session that you have stopped over-thinking and everything has become fluid, punch and counter punch, sequence and shuffle, bob and weave, instead of thinking of what you are doing you find yourself thinking of what your opponent is doing. Watching for his weak spots, spotting openings that you can use, watching the muscles in his shoulders slightly quiver and know with what seems like telepathic ability that a blow is coming your way, ducking and dodging to return the favour with your own flurry of blows. It's when these tactics come into play that you are startled with the realisation that you can now, with all confidence, call yourself a Boxer. With this realisation comes a responsibility that you need to do justice to your newly acquired title, and you know that you can only do this through fine-tuning your skill. A fusion of mind, body and soul you try to improve your stamina while widening your ability to deal with what you know you will face in competition, all the while keeping the mind set of dedication and perseverance. This whole exercise leading to the one goal of confidently facing a stranger across 24 feet of canvas. Two gladiators pitting their skill against one another.

They day of competition comes and you begin to wonder have you done enough to prepare, you could do with another couple of weeks just to give you the edge, what if he has trained more. Shaking your head you banish these confidence-shattering thoughts you begin reciting a litany of self-help phrases. 'I can do this. I can do this.' 'Power and speed. Power and speed.' This internal mantra drowning out the voice of coach as he goes through his own pre-fight speech. The excitement of the moment begins manifesting itself in your inability to sit still, pacing, bouncing and grunting all punctuated by sporadic bursts of hyper-tensive shadow boxing. A head popping into the dressing room announces that your fight is up next causing the butterflies that you had been so diligently trying to quell, quadruple in intensity. The coach grabs you and sits you on the bench checking your hands once more and telling you how great you are, how fast and how strong. It has the desired effect, the moment is now upon you, you feel the tension drain from you, replaced by resolve, no point in fighting the inevitable now 'Power and speed. Power and speed.' Strange moments in your training flit through your mind, skipping, working the speedball, and wiping the sweat off your face. Concentrate, you tell yourself.

The cheers and catcalls of the crowd are only brushing the edges of your focus; all you can see is the ring that you are being led towards. Climbing in you remember how you told yourself to behave, you put on your best intimidating look while also trying to look bored, confident and unscared at the same time, hoping you are pulling it off. The ring MC introduces you and you raise your arms in acknowledgement, and then turn your back when the same is done for your opponent. He's beneath your notice.

Where is the time going? Ding - ding. Here goes, everything on autopilot, he's dropping his guard on my left, he's open on my right when he jabs, he telescopes the haymakers, oh Christ caught me that was a good right, get back, recover, right here goes. Ding – ding. Is that two minutes already, what was I worried about, I'm enjoying this. Coach is talking; listen to him, ok got it. Ding – ding. Here we go again, 'Power and speed. Power and speed.'

Ding – ding... Ding – ding... Ding – ding...

It's over, wow. Looking out, the ref holds my hand as he waits to give the result. I see for what seems to be the first time the crowd in the hall, a couple of hundred people have just watched me fight, bemused I look around to see if I can see my Mum and Dad, maybe I can gauge how well I done from their faces. But before I can spot them half the crowd jumps up and everybody is applauding. I look to my left and only then see that it is my hand being held up by the ref. I've won, oh God I've won. I jump up and punch the air only to be caught by coach who holds me up there while I raise my arms in victory. The crowds are still cheering; I can now spot my parents the look on their faces is all I could have hoped for. The next few minutes are a blur as I'm ushered back to the dressing room; the unreality of it broken by claps on the back and loudly voiced congratulations. Could anything feel as good as this?

I'm a Boxer and I'm proud.

A Bewley's boy

Jimmy Curran

The closing of the doors on Bewley's runs shivers down me, as if a member of my family was passing away.

As a young boy in the 50s I grew up living on the very premises in Fleet St/Westmoreland St in Dublin. My father was the caretaker so living on the top floor meant we had a three bedroom flat, as they were called in those days. As a bonus we had a playground on the roof which was flat and totally fenced in overlooking the city.

As children my two brothers and I had many advantages over other children, for example we could sit and look out our window at the Easter and Saint Patrick's day parades, to the envy of many children standing below in the streets.

My father started work each day at 05.30AM, lighting very big boilers down in the basement; these boilers were fuelled by coke, a type of coal not to be confused with the drink.

It had to be shovelled into the boilers by hand; these boilers supplied heat and hot water to the building.

He then would let the bakers and confectionary workers in as they arrived at 06:00am.

The building in Fleet St /Westmoreland St was a mass of underground passageways leading from one street to the next. It consisted of the kitchens and coal room, where the coal was delivered through a hole in the street above. There was an electrician's and plumbers work shop.

As a child playing through these passage-ways was a magical world to be in, in the simple times of the 50s and 60s. I awoke every morning to the sound of two gigantic dough mixers in the bake-house mixing for the fresh bread to supply the Bewley's shops.

The sweet factory was a schoolboy's dream. Everything was made by hand by very skilled workers who prided themselves in their work. At the end of each day employees could purchase cakes, and bread at a third of the price. I can remember the cherry buns, almond buns, coffee cakes, walnut cakes.

These are most beautiful memories that will never leave my mind.

I remember Mr. Victor and Mr. Alfred Bewley, always referred to as Mr. Victor or Mr. Alfred.

Mr. Victor would often travel to Kenya to visit coffee farms and purchase supplies for the following year. On his arrival he would show slides of his trip to the staff in the café in Westmoreland St. I can remember going to see these slides in the days when there was very little television around, so it was a great thrill to be given this night out from Mr. Victor.

I was often very proud to see my dad standing in the window in Westmoreland St. roasting the same coffee I had seen on the slides with Mr Victor. I was brought to the Bewley farm in Ballydowd on the back of my dad's motor bike to see the Jersey herd, whose milk was used in the cafes and bakery. The café was often used to make many films, I recall one Sunday afternoon a film crew being in there for the whole day filming. I can't remember the film but the main star was Peter Finch.

As it had been a very busy day for everyone on the set, my father decided to ask Peter Finch to have a drink with him in his local "The Palace Bar" in Fleet St. Unknown to my mother my dad had overstayed his time with his new acquaintance. There were ten flights of stairs 13 steps in each so as people made their way they could be heard making their way up or down. The footsteps were soon to be heard, they were almost at the top when my father's voice rang out "wait till see who I have with me". My mother I think was saying in her mind wait till you see what I have for you.

When the door opened and in walked the two stars of the "Palace Bar" my mother almost passed away. Peter was three sheets to the wind; he was welcomed and made roast beef sandwiches to soak up the beer that had been well tanked. As a kid I was very proud to sit and watch a film star eat Monday's dinner. That was one of my funniest memories.

Sadly we had to endure two very bad fires in our time there and were lucky to escape one that ocurred in the early hours of the morning. We had to be taken down from the building by fire ladder as the flames lashed the building. The building was badly destroyed and we had to move out for some time while it was being refurbished. We were left with little or nothing. Thankfully no life was lost in either of the fires.

As a young boy I became very observant of the famous people that passed in and out of Bewley's from Abbey actors to writers, stars of radio, and films. I can remember one night in March 1966 going to bed like any other night with the neon signs flashing on the walls of my bedroom. Only to be awoken by a very loud explosion, it was Nelson's Pillar being blown to bits.

I took the army coat of the bed and made my way across to O'Connell St. with my dad to witness the damage and gather some of the rock. Which was presented to the odd tourist in the "Palace Bar" on many occasions?

The world was a different place in those days, but living in Bewley's was a very special place to be. To the many people who worked for the original Bewley's they will remember the employer who had a caring, considerate and very Christian attitude to their staff. To the remaining members of the Bewley family whom I have felt a part of I say thank you for what you gave to Dublin and my dad.

Finally in June 1973 at the age of 52 years my dad died very suddenly on a Sunday morning.

Being a man of those times he did not believe in life insurance or investments so we were left with nothing. As the dwelling went with my dad's job my mother had to deal with the loss of a husband, father, bread winner and the very roof over our head. Shortly after my father's funeral Mr. Victor contacted my mother to call the family together. This was a very worrying time for her. Mr. Victor soon put her at ease. At the family meeting he made her an offer that no employer would do in this day and age.

He told her to take the family and go choose a house where ever she liked. He told her he was giving her a loan totally interest free over any amount of time to be paid back whatever way she choose. With nothing in writing.

As a family my mother had been thrown a life line by the Bewley family in a most Christian gesture. My mother bought a house in the north of the city and worked hard to pay back her payments. Such was the speed of her repayments Mr. Victor would not take some of the final payments.

This again was another Christian gesture by Mr Victor. On top of that she received a widow's pension from the company and her Christmas hamper every year, and her pensioner's party. My mother has now passed on, but the Bewley's memories live on with my brothers and me, for the rest of our days.

Simple days in many ways and memories to cherish.

OUR FIRST TOURISTS WENT BY CANAL

John Cassidy

The average person would find it difficult to believe if told today that the Grand Canal Company were the pioneers of the tourist traffic in Ireland and if one added they built luxurious hotels on the banks of this ancient and famous waterway he or she would shake their heads and say what an incredible story, but the fact is it is quite true.

Thousands of passengers travelled over the canal more than one hundred and fifty years ago and were housed in what were then, no doubt, luxury hotels. The first hotel was built at Portobello in the year 1807 at a cost of eleven thousand pounds. There were other hotels built at Sallins, Robertstown, Tullamore and Shannon Harbour, but the Portobello hotel would appear to have been built to last for all time. The stone in the building came from Tullamore and the slates from Killaloe and the chimney pieces from marble quarries in Offaly.

The charge in those far off days for breakfast with egg was one shilling and eight pence, dinner two shillings and two pence, tea or coffee one shilling and a room three shillings and six pence. In all eight shillings and one penny per day; I can hear tourists say "those were the days."

The hotel at Sallins was erected in 1785 and the hotel at Robertstown was completed at a cost of seven thousand pounds. The Tullamore hotel cost four thousand pounds, and in 1805 the hotel at Shannon Harbour was erected for five thousand pounds.

It is on the record that the Catholic Church at Tullamore had to be enlarged because of the influx of passengers carried by the canal to this progressive midland town.

Lord Dunboyne was appointed Inspector of passenger boats at the handsome salary of eight hundred pounds per year. Charles Bianconi, the founder of public transport in Ireland, ran a road service to meet the arrival of boats at certain points and convey the passengers to their destination. Boats ran day and night, each boat had a first and second class cabin and was swiftly towed along the canal by two horses. In those remote days it was necessary to arm the masters or captains of the boats with pistols as protection against highway men and robbers.

During the rebellion of 1798 the government commandeered all the passenger boats to convey military and stores to Tullamore from Dublin. When the French landed at Killala in County Mayo, Lord Cornwallis embarked with a large number of troops and baggage on the boats and hastened as far as Tullamore from which place the troops marched to meet the enemy.

Napper Tandy (immortalised in the song "the wearing of the green") and Robert Emmet's father were co-directors of the Company. The Grand Canal was the premier method of transport and it carried one hundred thousand passengers annually. The boats were nicely fitted with bars and dining rooms, with staff in attendance, and the spoons served with meals were solid silver.

The passenger on the Shannon was served by two large paddle boats named the Lady Lansdowne and the Lady Burgoyne. These steamers plied between Kilaloe and Athlone and Bianconi's cars left Limerick each morning with mostly emigrants to meet the boats at Killaloe.

In the year 1852 the Canal Company found it no longer profitable to continue running their passenger boats and ceased doing so after a long and glorious career lasting seventy years.

THE PHOTOGRAPH

Angela Macari

It was the last week in November and I was making a Christmas cake. Suddenly an incoming text made me jump. I cursed the interruption, stopped what I was doing and looked at the message.

It was Angie, a former school pal I hadn't seen in fifteen years. She had met my sister and asked if she could have my number. I was shocked, but elated too as I read the text. She wanted to call me, but was unsure if it was a good moment. It wasn't but I feared that if I didn't respond, I might never hear from her again. So, I said 'Yes, call me please!'

Tears flowed as I listened to a voice I thought I'd never hear again. We talked of our lives. She mentioned that she was moving away from Dublin in a week. How sad we had only rediscovered each other and she was moving away. We arranged to meet and when the day arrived I was very excited, wondering would I recognise her. But I needn't have worried, for there outside Trinity College stood my friend, a little older but with the same big smile and blonde hair. We hugged and soon made our way to 'The Bank', her favourite place. We ordered lunch and chatted, exchanging updates about characters from our mutual patch, the Liberties. So much had changed. There were sad tales of chums who died and happier ones too. Angie updated me on some of our old teachers with whom she kept in touch. The afternoon flew by and as we tottered to our buses, we vowed to meet again.

When Angie had settled into her new home, I went for a visit. On a frosty December day, I drove to her beautiful new house to meet her partner and family. I was given the red carpet treatment and a sumptuous dinner. Again we talked and she showed me around her lovely town, stopping off for a drink or two. I returned the invitation and just before Christmas, Angie came to me and met my husband, son and my two dear cats. Life was changing for me now that I'd found a piece of my youth and a vital link in the chain of my life.

A few months passed before I saw Angie again. I met another girl from the Liberties, one evening while shopping, I spotted her at the checkout and I touched her arm as she was going towards her car. As soon as she recognised me, she threw her arms around me. Grainne had been at school with Angie and me. We hadn't been close, but I always liked her. We exchanged numbers and email addresses. She asked had I met anyone from our old area and I told her about Angie. She was intrigued and said she had been trying to organise a school reunion for years.

After a few emails, texts and some planning, the three of us met at Angie's house on a Sunday afternoon. During the laughter, stories and a delicious feast of lasagne, followed by strawberries, Grainne showed us some old photographs. She asked if I could see myself. I searched for a minute and soon spotted my dark hair, with my white ribbon, my partially hidden face among forty five innocent, wide eyed six year olds. I vaguely remembered some and tried to remember names.

At the back of the group stood our nun, the Maria Von Trapp of Warren Mount Convent, her hands joined gracefully and a smile on her face. Sr.Therese was an angel. We had her in senior infants for only a few months. Rumour has it that she fell in love and left the convent to get married. At home that night I looked at the black and white picture of my class. I still can't remember them all. I spotted one bully, who often pinched me. How tiny and innocent she looks to me now. I also saw Grainne in the front row, beside the other Grainne who was an equally beautiful girl. They were known as the two Grainnes and we were the two Angies.

It's a piece of the jigsaw of my life, this one from forty years ago. This photograph has given me inspiration, because it holds memories of childhood that were obliterated, when I lost my home in a tragic fire in 1986. This, like many of my experiences carved me into who I am today and the once shy six year old in the photograph, now drives a double deck bus. Who would have guessed? Each time I look, I recognise one more face and say a little prayer for her wherever she is. Maybe they do the same for me!

TRAIN-JACKED

Thomas Carroll

" I went to bed at twenty past nine last night and listened to the radio; it's much better than the television" John said, as the early morning train passed by fields covered in a blanket of snow.

"You're much better than I am; at least you manage to get into bed early. Me, I'm up half the night watching DVD's. You know how mad into movies I am," Mike said. John smiled as the food and snack trolley approached.

"Don't know how Laura ever puts up with me. Guess she really does love me, warts and all," Mike said as he sipped his too hot coffee. Suddenly the interior lights of the train went dark. The darkness only lasted five seconds, like going through a short tunnel. When the lights returned the man who was pushing the tea trolley was holding a semi-automatic.

"Alright, everyone just stay calm and stay sitting where you are. Don't move from your seats and no one will get hurt," said the man in a very military voice. He levelled the weapon just above his waistline. A woman sitting in front of John and Mike began to cry and sob out loud. Another man carrying a semi-automatic came through the walkway from the next carriage and offered the woman a tissue.

"This train will not be going to Grand Central. Instead we'll be taking a slight detour to Chicago," the first man said. "You may talk amongst yourselves and feel free to have refreshments from the tea trolley. But before you do anything I want everyone to hand over their mobile phones, wallets and any weapons."

"We're going to have to do something," Mike said in a low voice. "We can't just sit here and let these bastards take over."

"It's been a while since our military service in the Gulf and I'm not sure I want to tackle what sounds like ex-military people turned terrorists," John said.

"Don't worry, just stay calm and let's see if these punks have a weak spot or two," Mike said.

Night had fallen and the train continued on its diverted way towards Chicago. Some of the passengers had fallen asleep; while others were too worried to do so. The sight of an armed man in every carriage was more than enough to prevent the majority of people from getting some shuteye.

"I've figured a way of maybe putting the odds a bit more in our favour. See that tea trolley parked up at the end of the carriage. Well if one of us could poison the tea and coffee with something like Epsom salts, there is a high chance these dudes would get the shits like never before," John said as he eased four small sachets from inside his jacket.

"Yeah, but what about if some of the people drink the stuff as well. Won't that mean we could have one hell of a rush for the bathroom," Mike said with a touch of humour in his eyes.

"That's a chance were going to have to take. At least it's only super strong Epsom salts, not hydrochloric acid," John said. Suddenly the barrel of an automatic rifle was millimetres away from Mike's face.

"You two are doin' an awful lot of talkin'. How about you shut your traps and get some sleep," the terrorist said with a gruff voice. John and Mike both nodded and pretended to fall asleep. They should have known that professional soldiers usually cover every angle of opportunity. The Gulf and Afghan wars taught them that lesson. Like a lot of things in life, even soldiers can get rusty, especially off duty ones.

"I'm going to the bathroom. Jesus I can hardly hold it!" Mike said clutching his crotch. John looked at him in amusement.

"Excuse me, but I need to have a pee," Mike said to the man holding the automatic.

"Ok. Off you go bud. Don't spend too long in there." Once inside the tiny bathroom, Mike quickly opened the four sachets of extra strong Epsom salts and emptied their contents into his false bladder. The white flaky powder was now mixed with very yellow urine. It began to fizz with little bubbles of white froth. He also mixed in five small packets of salt. Mike smiled as he thought how potent this concoction would be. Before opening the bathroom door Mike readied himself for action. With a groan Mike staggered out of the little room. He was bent over both hands seeming to clutch his crotch. "Oh Christ I need a doctor", he winced.

"What's up ..." said the gunman looking bemused. But that was all he had time to say. Mike lunged upright and sprayed the foaming contents of his false bladder at the man. Instantly the gunman fell backwards firing his weapon at the ceiling which made the lights go out. Clutching his face he screamed obscenities at Mike.

"You fucking bastard I'll ..." John gave the man a sharp kick in the stomach which prevented him finishing his sentence. John swiped the gun from the floor and pointed it at the man who was in a state of agony as he held his hands over his face which had turned a raw red colour. The lights flickered on again but were not as bright this time. Suddenly glass exploded from the door behind Mike. The other gunman was running towards this carriage. Just as he reached the start of the carriage an old man put out his walking stick and sent the gunman crashing onto the floor. A live grenade rolled forward. Without hesitating the old man fell on top of it. There was a muffled thud as his body jumped slightly while absorbing the force of the explosion.

John was busy shooting at the third gunman who was getting closer to their carriage. Most of the windows had been shot out. The cold night's air blew in. Mike fired several rounds from the automatic he picked up when the second gunman had fallen. A woman who had been hiding in the bathroom rushed out screaming hysterically, bullets ripped into her back and front and for five seconds her body remained upright as both Mike and the gunman continued firing. Her bloodied body collapsed onto the floor; immediately the gunman's automatic jammed. Instantly Mike fired his weapon the man jolted back into a seat, blood pouring from his head. Several other people also lay slumped in their seats apparently killed in the shootout. The carriage was a mess of dead bodies and broken window glass; most of the lights were shot out. The remaining passengers in

Mike and John's carriage peered nervously over their seats and hoped the siege had come to an end.

But there was still one more gunman. He was holding the train driver hostage in the engine at the very front of the train.

"I'll take care of this one," John said as he hurriedly made his way out through a blown out window and onto the roof of the carriage.

"Be careful," Mike called after him. Bullets whizzed past John as he crawled along the roof of the locomotive. He could make out the shape of the gunman as he leaned out of the door of the train engine. John returned fire, missing the gunman each time. John was now directly over the cab. He knew he would have only one chance to get it right. All his special forces training had prepared him for moments like this. Swinging his body he shot into the cab feet first, catching the gunman in the face. The man almost fell out the other door of the cab. His automatic lay on the floor. Scooping up the weapon John fired point blank into the man's face. He disappeared into the dawn that had begun to break.

"You alright buddy?" John asked the terrified train driver who had sought refuge on the floor of the small cab.

"I'll survive. Got a few bruises, but I'll make it," said the driver as blood trickled from his nose and mouth. The train was brought to a safe stop and moments later police rescue teams along with TV cameras arrived.

Mike and John were both awarded medals for bravery by the US Army and were personally thanked by the train company for their quick thinking. The passengers were also grateful and John and Mike received many letters of appreciation for their bravery.

"Well I guess we're going to be famous from now on," Mike said smiling.

"Yeah, looks like it. But I think next time we have to go to a military reunion we had better drive. I don't fancy being train-jacked again. At least this sort of mayhem would be less likely to happen," John said as he cleaned the chamber of his Magnum 45.

Autumn day

Cathy Hickey

I am walking in the woods,
The Autumn wind takes the leaves from the trees,
They fall around me
And crunch beneath my feet.
I watch them dancing on the wind
And think of You.
You would wonder at this,
The sound of the river rushing by,
Breathing the sweet crisp air.
Absorbing the warmth of colour,
Enjoying the sight of a young squirrel
Busily preparing for Winter,
At the base of the magnificent old tree,
Simplistic, yet so complex,
This cycle of Life.......Nature.....
It saddens me to think, yet again,
You are missing this moment.
Then it occurs to me that you are not,
Because you are here, walking with me.
Sharing this joy!!!!!!!

THE BUS IS FOR US

Declan Gowran

It's Car Free day in Dublin and the buses are packed. Or should that read Bus Free day as Dublin Bus reclaims the streets? There's a little magic in the air and colour and pageantry as it is also the All-Ireland Football Finals day and the city is a tapestry of movement breathing an excited air of expectancy.

"It's your bus.....so are you still going to use it after all the fuss has died down, and it's no longer free?"

That is the question and such was the theme of the Tapestry EU initiative conducted among schoolchildren in the Coolock area recently. One of the slogans dreamt up by an inspired student provides the heading for this piece and an innovative advertisement displayed on the side of the number 27 bus.

In many ways children are among the wisest, cutest and sometimes the most cruel people in the world. Children invariably speak from the hip when they shoot their mouths off with a passion, and they say things as they see them. Their vision too can be inspiring as evidenced by the posters and poems submitted for the Tapestry competition. Fact is that every child who took part was a winner; but it was Dublin Bus that benefited most from the children's unstinting efforts and ideas.

Praise to all the children who took part and special praise should go to Peter Scott, Quality and Commercial Manager, Gerry Charles, Worker Director and local Clontarf workers' representative, and to Michael Mathews, Operations Manager, who took time out to become the real face of Dublin Bus when he presented the awards to the obviously delighted winners, in helping to organise and fulfil a wonderful scheme of customer involvement.

For many years Dublin Bus has visited junior schools in the Dublin area to familiarise young people with the ethos of the bus as a vital cog in the machinery of everyday life. It served to illustrate the importance of the bus in everyday life and why vehicles and crews should be treated with the respect and safety that such a vital service deserves. The former and the newer bus commercials devised under the auspices of Bronagh Rooney as Marketing Manager serve to develop this theme in the most potent of ways through the medium of television where the human face of Dublin Bus comes to life as ordinary staff are seen performing their duties. People as passengers appreciate that staff in Dublin Bus do a professional job often under trying conditions and the majority are willing to give the company a chance despite upsets caused by traffic. The staff itself is always willing to cover manpower shortages or give their services to special events and shuttles as witnessed at Slane and the recent Family Day in the Phoenix Park. In that regard it would be futile and inflammatory for the Government of the day to even contemplate the breaking-up or the privatising of what has become in later years a most efficient Dublin Bus company. Diversification can lead to chaos. Children especially recognise this. Signs are so important to them as well as logos. The bus they catch to school should always be recognisable too with an invariably friendly driver at the wheel. We all have our moments, and children will be children, sometimes noisy and rough and ready. But we were all children once and most respond favourably to a firm but friendly command.

Children like to be treated as equals. Children are clever and can see through fabrication.

In this way the Tapestry initiative has been so important and enlightening. Put it this way: 'We have all grown up a bit, even Dublin Bus'. We have shown that we care for our children's opinions and they have responded in such a magnificent way. We have learned so much more now about each other that we can progress onto further plateaux of excellence.

Hopefully the old spates of window smashing by stone throwing children will become a bad memory of the past for now after all if the throwers cast their stones they will only be defacing the efforts of their peers and schoolmates and that would be simply unforgiveable.

The tapestry advertisements on the side of the 27 bus are a testament to the future success of community partnership and Dublin Bus. Despite accusations of inefficiency and an uncaring nature Dublin Bus has always liaised with its public, and has done so admirably with this Tapestry initiative. It's always great to have an idea for improvement; but it is so more important to put ideas into practice. That's how the world moves on.

Wisdom is such a great attribute in a person, even more so in a public company. In children Dublin Bus recognises its customers of the future and knows they should be involved in transport development, their ideas nurtured, analysed and acted upon in order to provide an even better quality bus service. In turn it shouldn't surprise anybody that from this Tapestry initiative some super advertisement and marketing executives of the future will be driven in their chosen careers, and yes, maybe even a bus driver or two.

Bloomsday

Ronnie Hickey

By swerve of hip
And click of heel
From Grafton Street
To College Green
Slowly sways
The denimmed haunches
Silken warm
Caressing blouse
Yellow ribboned
Shining hair
Dances into
Bobbing heads
Of multicoloured
Hurrying crowd
Found and lost
One summer bloomtime
Swells and delights
The fading heart.

THE BOOK WORM

Scotty Sturgeon

I'm a bookworm. You see me everywhere, in the theatre, reading the play at the interval, in the park huddled over a digest, and if you peep over my shoulder in the bus you will see me devouring the editorials. My favourite haunt is the local library and even though you see me do not expect me to recognise you, for I am far away in dim horizons cleaving my way through the Amazon jungle, or maybe intent on 'who done it.'

Books are my friends and faithful companions. There's always one with me, naturally I like some better than others, and each day the circle widens. Practically every sphere of knowledge comes within my orbit, travel, science, fiction, philosophy, anthropology and in fact every ology you can think of. I understand people because I am always reading about them, psychology is a fascinating hobby, pin-point the various neuroses that affect mankind, and then look for them in your friends. Sometimes I think there is not one completely normal person alive.

I have been everywhere, met all the famous people who ever lived, enjoyed their thoughts, seen the marvels of science, the discoveries of medicine and the pomp and pageantry of history.

I was with Cleopatra as she sailed down the Nile to meet Anthony. I laughed with Nero at the burning of Rome, and heard the mighty Coliseum resound to the yells of the blood thirsty rabble. I followed the Greeks to Troy, I watched the pagan fires die out over Europe and its cathedrals rise to the skies.

I visited the four corners of the world, I crossed the Atlantic with Columbus, I was with Livingstone in Africa, and Scott at the South Pole. I saw the blood-drenched altars of the Incas, Marie Antoinette ascending to the guillotine, I was present at the Gettysburg address, the attack on Pearl Harbour and saw the atom bomb descending on Hiroshima, witnessed famines and wars in every corner of the world. I have won and lost elections, played in every major sporting event imaginable.

The music of words infected me and I was swept along by them into the fantastic lands of poetry. What one of you have not succumbed to the beauty of Omar Khayyam's verse, enjoy life he says; forget the past and live only for the present; the pursuit of knowledge is futile, profit by the example of bygone sages as 'their words to scorn are scattered, and their mouths are stopt with dust.'

They say books are only a reflection of life that they should serve as an example to a better concept of living. But books are not the background of my life, they are my life, and occasionally I wonder if I am missing something. I read mostly about people, and how they served the society in which they lived. A book, a chair by the fireside and imagination peeping over my shoulder is all I ask, but I cannot prevent these uneasy thoughts bubbling in my mind.

What will the recording Angel write about me in the book of life? Will he accept a list of the books I have read, or will he question my deeds? There's that parable of the Ten Talents and the man who buried his talents in the earth....

That's the worst of reading, it always sets you thinking.

THE GERIATRIC WARD

Thomas Carroll

The geriatric ward in Mount Temple Hospital was no different to any other geriatric ward you are likely to find in any other hospital. The patients were on their last legs, just waiting for life to run out. Sam Smith was one of the oldest patients in the ward. He was seventy-seven and if truth be told, he didn't feel like giving up on life just yet. Sam had spent his life in the army; always wanted to get into the SAS. Had it not been for stomach trouble and his tendency to make extremely loud farts, well who knows? He might have been another Andy McNabb perhaps. But then life doesn't always deal out the cards that make everything go to plan. He got an office job and became personal secretary to a high ranking colonel. Sam liked this work; at least it meant that he got home every night to be with his wife and their two children, Sophie and Peter.

What the other people in the ward didn't know was that Sam had an ability to perform magic. Not just cheap skate hocus-pocus stuff, but real serious disappearing type magic. Sam always carefully chose his time to use this magic so that nobody would ever suspect him. He didn't want to be labelled a freak or the next David Blaine. You see Sam knew he was never going to die. About twenty years ago he began to develop a special potion that would prevent him from ever going beyond the age of seventy-seven. This 'live forever potion' had to be drunk once a week so that the body and mind would be prevented from ageing. The only trouble now was that Sam would have to get to his flat at the other side of the city so that he could make the potion. Getting out of Mount Temple geriatric ward was no easy matter. He was going to have to get hold of a doctor's surgery coat or some disguise so as to escape.

Sam arrived at his flat and with the utmost speed set about preparing the 'live forever potion'. He mixed the ingredients in a big cooking bowl and placed this in the oven to cook for three hours. The smell alone is pretty strong; luckily the extractor fan takes care of this. When the stuff was cooked Sam allows it to cool before eating half of the substance. It looked like a big cake, but it certainly didn't taste like cake, more like sea weed. How he was ever going to get one of the other patients to eat this stuff was going to be a real challenge. He would have to sweeten the ingredients with honey and use vanilla flavouring to subdue the overpowering smell – a smell that was not unlike cat's urine along with salty sea water!

When Jim Richards bit into his dinner that day little did he realise that the contents had been deliberately invested with 'live forever potion'. The fact that his dinner was slightly sweeter than usual didn't cause him undue concern; in fact the sweet taste was a change from the bland food that was usually served. Even his tea tasted slightly sweeter. Jim was seventy-one and one day soon he would thank Sam most graciously for the gift of eternal life he was now secretly bestowing upon him even if it was going to give Jim the heaviest bout of diarrhoea he would ever experience in his long life.

BOOTSIE

Declan Gowran

You know what they say about men with big feet? They have to get their shoes specially made by the cobbler. Made to measure from toes to heels to insteps to ankles with the appropriate allowances made for the type of sock to be worn. This factor of course would also depend on the seasons and whether the wearer's feet were prone to sweating. Style might also enter the equation; but at the time that I'm going to talk about, the good old- fashioned leather brogues were the boots to be seen in. These brogues were all leather tops, soles and heels with indented patterns and overlapping strips that suggested a sturdy bulkiness that would suit the cobbles of the farmyard or the polished floor of the Ceili House.

The only trouble was it was expensive to have your own shoes made especially if you happened to be a bus driver back in the Hungry Sixties.

During the Sixties the first OMO buses were introduced. These were One Man Operated and came with a premium of an extra 20% over and above the basic wages of the day. Some new routes like Coolock started off as single-deck OMO operated services while others like the North Wall were developed. Because of the extra wages involved the more senior of the drivers were to be found manning these OMO routes on a marked-in basis while others might work a rest-day as an OMO if they had undergone the training.

About this time a driver in Clontarf called Footsie found himself working on the North Wall. Footsie was aptly named because this guy had massive clogs for feet. Footsie was big in other ways too. He was a particularly big hit with the ladies who were attracted by his dexterity around the dance floor. He would literally sweep them off their feet by standing them up on his huge insteps as he glided round the floor. They were equally impressed on the walk home afterwards particularly if there was any lovers' lane handy on the route where Footsie might demonstrate some other of his big attributes.

Footsie used to have his boots specially made. This was an expensive business so much so that Footsie could only afford to have one pair of brogues to be made at one time. These boots were always black so that they would match his uniform. As a consequence most of his civvies were in darker colours to go with the boots. It was always Footsie's dream and ambition to have a pair of brown brogues so that he could expand his wardrobe. If only he could afford the extra pair. It may have been one reason why he worked OMO.

Just after Christmas one year Footsie was working the last North Wall. He had a fair load on for the B&I Boat as many of the emigrant workers and navvies were heading back to Blighty after spending the Christmas with their families. After pulling into Clontarf Garage and parking the bus Footsie, while making his cursory last check for lost property, discovered a big hunk of a country lad crouched into the corner of the back seat dead asleep to the world and obviously a bit worse for wear from the drink. Cradled on his lap in his arms was his bag of belongings. The bag rose and fell like a gentle tide with his steady breathing.

"Wake-up son!" Footsie called out as he shook the young lad. "You've arrived whether you like it or not!"

The young lad, startled by Footsie's massive shake, blurted out:

"Have we landed then...show me the way to the London train..."

"'Tis a long way from London ye are son, more nearer to Tipperary in fact!"

"Wha! Where am I? Where's this?"

Footsie calmly explained as the young lad got unsteadily to his feet.

"Ah no!" The young lad sighed: " Wha' time is it? If I miss that boat McAlpine'll have me life! Please ye got to help me! Get me to the boat on time! I'll give ye anything! Name yer price! Pleaaaase!"

Footsie looked him up and down. He felt sorry for the poor bugger. Then he noticed the young lad's feet or more properly the lovely spanking brand new brown leather brogues that the young lad was wearing.

"Here!" Footsie commanded: " Ger up and stand beside me for a minute…"

"As I thought." Footsie grinned with satisfaction: "Sure I'll get you to the boat, son, but just on one condition."

Footsie pulled the bus out of the garage and drove hell bent for rubber to catch the B&I Boat for the young navvy. They made it with minutes to spare before the gangplank was raised.

"I'm mightily obliged to you, sir!" The young lad said gratefully before parting.

"Sure it's nothing son," Footsie replied, feeling a little guilty: "So 'tis alright about the shoes then…."

"No bother!" The young lad said sincerely: "Think of them as a belated Christmas present!"

The young lad boarded the boat; but nobody seemed to notice that he walked up the gangplank in his stocking feet.

When Footsie got home he couldn't wait to try on his new Christmas brogues:

"Just as I thought," He smiled with satisfaction: "Made to measure! A perfect fit!"

AND ALL HIS SONGS WERE SAD

(A Full-length Play)

Mattie Lennon

SCENE ONE
Time; 1937.

Set; A stretch of country road in late autumn as day-light is fading. Centre back is a small open shed with straw bedding and dying foliage on either side. It contains a milking-stool.

(A middle-aged man with clay on his boots and carrying a spade enters from R. Two boys aged about fourteen, Willie McSweeney and the more precocious Sean McCarthy, enter from L.
They meet centre stage)

MAN:	Good evening to yis both.
WILLIE:	Have you them all dug?
Man :	Almost.
Willie:	How far is it to Limerick?
MAN:	(without" breaking his step") Twenty-six statute miles.
SEAN;	When a stranger tells you how far we have to go will you believe him?Will we lie down here? It's getting dark and my feet are sore.
WILLIE:	My feet are sore too, we must be after walking thirty mile.
SEAN:	It's not thirty miles from Listowel to Newcastlewest.
WILLIE:	How far is it?
SEAN:	Well. It's six miles to Duagh. It's another four and a half to Abbeyfeale, and twelve and a half from Abbeyfeale to here. Twenty-three miles altogether.

WILLIE: Well aren't you the smart fellow.

SEAN: *(Sitting down on milking-stool, milking an imaginary cow in time to the tune as he sings)*
             I'm intelligent Sean McCarthy.
             An' I'm known to all the boys,
             I live at the foot of Haley's wood
             With muck up to my eyes.

WILLIE: You made that up didn't you?

SEAN :   I wrote that, Willie, when I was seven years old. But I did get a bit of help from the Tailor Roche.

WILLIE: What was that rhyme that you got slapped for saying in school?

SEAN: That was written by Paddy Drury from Knockanure. Paddy was working for the Vicar. And the Vicar's housekeeper, Kate Nealon, according to Paddy, kept her loins exceptionally well girded (even by the standards of the day) and out of bounds to Paddy. Then Paddy found himself jobless when he expressed his bewilderment and frustrations in verse,
             Kate Nealon's virtue remains intact
`   **Tis locked up hard and tight.**
             One puzzling aspect of that fact,
             How does she piss at night?

WILLIE: You were always different. You always noticed things that the rest of us missed. Maybe that's what the School-Master meant when he said that you were special.

SEAN;   I suppose everyone is special in their own way. But if you don't play football in Galvin's field and pitch-and-toss on the Forge road you're considered a sissy. My brother Mick always said I was a dreamer; that I was going around in a daze.

WILLIE;   What does Mick think of you going to join the army?

SEAN;   He doesn't know, he's in London. But I don't think he'd mind me joining the Irish Army, sure he went to join the Free State army himself. Then when he got there recruiting was closed down for Easter. Oh, he was too cute to tramp to Limerick. He hopped on the train when it stopped at the level-crossing and stowed away. He once threatened all sorts of things on me if I ever even thought of joining the British Army.

WILLIE; I didn't think Mick was like that.

SEAN; He's not. A girl he was great with was after being drowned in Bundoran. The Doctor said he had a nervous breakdown.

WILLIE; He still wouldn't want you to join the English Army?

SEAN; Three years before I was born the Black-and-Tans kicked down the door of the house at my grandmother's wake and shot the little dog. Mick was there. He remembers that. And another night they nearly shot him and my father.

WILLIE; And that made him turn against the English.

SEAN; It did an' it didn't. In the first letter he sent home he told my mother how kind the English people were and about how a London cop had given him half-a-crown.

WILLIE;(*losing interest in what Sean is saying)* You that's good at sums....what year would you have to be born to be seventeen now.

SEAN; Nineteen twenty....why?

WILLIE; When we tell the army people in Limerick we're seventeen they might try to catch us out.*(Both take off their boots and sit down on the straw and there is silence for a few moments)*

WILLIE; *(Suddenly)* Is it true that girls go for fellows in uniform?

SEAN; I don't know much about girls or what they go for. Although my uncle, the Tumbler McCarthy, gave me a bit of advice about them but I can't vouch for the validity of it. I think he was a bit hard on the fairer sex. Do you know what a man that doesn't like women is called?

35

WILLIE:	No. What?
SEAN:	A Misogynist.
WILLIE:	*(Not impressed)* What did the Tumbler tell you?
SEAN:	The Tumbler was a man that spoke in Parables. He said, " Remember Seaneen, be careful of the mule with the calm look. You know what to expect from the mule with the mad eyes, but the hoor with the docile eyes will kick you when your mind is on other things".
WILLIE:	I suppose you'll write a song about this some time. Or can you write about hardship?
SEAN;	Of course you can. According to Shelley; Most wretched men are cradled into poetry by wrong. **They learn in suffering what they teach in song.** And didn't Dickens write about hardship?
WILLIE;	If his feet were skinned from traipsing the roads to get away from the hunger and bogs of North Kerry he mightn't be so fond of the pen.
SEAN;	Whatever about the hunger, the bog is part of us. You don't grow up in the bog....you grow up with the bog. It's not so much a place...it's .....more of a feeling.
WILLIE;	A feeling? What sort of a feeling.
SEAN:	I don't know, but it's there. *(Thoughtfully)* I think no matter where I'm posted in the army, in my head, I'll still hear the wild geese over Lyrocrompane and the trout jumping in the Cashen. When the wind howls at night it seems to be calling to me and wanting to tell me something....a tormented wind begging to be listened to.
WILLIE:	How would the wind be tormented and want to be listened to?
SEAN:	Sure tormented people want to be listened to. Maurice Walshe, the writer from Ballydonoghue, had it summed up.
WILLIE:	How?
SEAN:	He wrote, " A place acquires an entity of its own, an

entity that is the essence of all the life and thoughts
and griefs and joys that have gone before".
I know what he means. In my own case how could
I ever forget things like the sheer, lunacy of the
Rambling House that I experienced as a barefoot
child? The stories of people like the Whisper Hogan
and the lilting of "Doodlededom". They're things
that a person would carry with them for........

*(Sean looks over and sees the Willie is asleep. He finds a cigarette
        packet in the straw, tears it open, produces a stump
        of a pencil, and starts to write. As he is writing, in
        his head he can hear his own voice singing "Blow
        The Candles Out" .*

*There is a mansion on the hill where my love does reside,
Through the windows I do watch, I see my love inside.
I am cold and hungry, my aching heart does shout,
Oh, come into my arms love and we'll blow the candles out.*

*The door it silent opens and my love comes to me,
I do rush to his arms and hold him tenderly.
One stolen hour all in the night, he cries my name aloud,
Oh, take me in your arms love and we'll blow the candles out.*

*His mother she does slight me for I am not his kind,
I have no courtly manners and am I nor refined.
The waiting stars up in the sky, they pass by a cloud,
Take me in your arms.....................*

*(As twilight slowly turns to darkness he lies down and the song
        fades out)*

CURTAIN.

SCENE TWO.
Set; The same as in scene one.

(It's the next day. Willie and Sean enter from Stage R. looking dirtier and more travel-worn than the evening before)

WILLIE: How far would you say we walked since this time
             yesterday?

Sean: Thirty-five miles if you subtract the distance between
             Newcastlewest and Patrickswell, where we got the lift
             with the blacksmith.

WILLIE: You'd nearly be better walking than listening to his
             blather.

SEAN: Ah, he was very interesting. I could listen to him all
             day....The story about the Troubles.....how young
             Willie was shot in that town in West Limerick.
             That would be a lovely line in a song, "He died in
             Shanagolden on a lonely summer's night ". (*Sings*)

**And you fought them darling Willie all through the summer days
I heard the rifles firing in the mountains far away
I held you in my arms love and your blood ran free and bright
And you died by Shanagolden on a lonely summer's night.**

WILLIE: There's no fear of us being shot in action anyway,
             even our own army wouldn't have us. It was a wasted
             journey.

SEAN;   It's hard to know when anything is wasted. We
             learned something.

WILLIE;   Oh we did. We learned that you should have worn
             a long trousers for a week or a fortnight before
             you tried that trick. The minute you dropped your
             brother Mick's trousers for the medical examination
             your man knew by your weather-beaten legs that you
             weren't long out of short trousers. Seventeen how are
             you!

	(Sean looks pensive)
WILLIE;	What's wrong with you?
SEAN;	I have an ache.
WILLIE:	I'm sore all over. That was a long walk. We're not used to walking that far in one go.
SEAN:	Not that kind of an ache; an ache in my brain.
WILLIE:	A headache?
SEAN:	Not quite. An ache to write a song that will be published...and sung....especially sung *(dreamily)* Or to have a record made of one of my songs. Imagine what it must be like to be passing a house, maybe miles from home, and to hear your song played on the gramophone.
WILLIE:	Do you think that will ever happen?
SEAN:	It's not likely to happen in Kerry anyway. When I was still in school I wrote this song "Horo My Johnny". And when I asked O'Leary in Listowel to print it he said," ....waste o' time, who in the name of Christ wants to horo my Johnny.
WILLIE:	What sort of a song was it?
	(Sean sings "Horo My Johnny")

Chorus;
Oh! Horo my Johnny will you come home soon,
The winter is coming and I'm all alone.
The candle is burning in my window low,
And the wild geese they are going home.

A young man's love is something to behold,
First it burns and then it soon grows cold.
He'll whisper in the moonlight and your hand he'll hold,
Then he'll vanish like the morning dew.

Chorus.
He'll court you by a meadow in the summertime,
When first you love it is the sweetest time.
He'll promise you a golden ring and then one day,
He'll vanish like the morning dew.

You'll be waiting for his footsteps in a lonely room,
Listen by the window he'll be coming soon.
Your heart it will be breaking by the early dawn,
For he's vanished with the morning dew.

Chorus.
So come all you young men who are in your prime,
A young maiden's love is like the rarest wine.
When first you taste it 'tis a golden time,
And sweeter than the morning dew.

WILLIE:	What sort of things can you make a song about?
SEAN:	You can compose a song about anything.
WILLIE:	This road?
SEAN:	Yes....I suppose so.
WILLIE:	But this is the road to nowhere.
SEAN:	*(Brightening up)* That's great., *(Sings)*
	The Road to Nowhere turned dark with ugly alien gore
	The Quiet Man was dreaming of the Key Above the Door.
WILLIE:	What's that about?
SEAN:	It's about a couple of things. It's acknowledging the titles of the works of Maurice Walshe, the man that I told you about yesterday. And more importantly it's about our search.
WILLIE:	Our search ....for what?
SEAN:	I don't know. We don't always know what we're searching for. I saw in the Reader's Digest where Albert Einstein said, "If I knew what I was looking for it wouldn't be called research".
WILLIE:	You read a lot. I can't settle down to read.
SEAN:	There are many ways of reading; it's not all about books. You can listen, that's a form of reading. You can read the seasons and the landscape... And people. Most of all you can read people. You can learn everything from people. James Joyce says that he never met a boring person.

WILLIE:	He didn't spend much time around Listowel then.
SEAN:	Listowel has no boring people. It has kind people and it has nasty people. It has clever people and people that are not so clever. But we can learn something from them all.
WILLIE:	A lot of them say that you have a great imagination.
SEAN:	I think I got it from my mother's side. My uncle, the Salmon Roche, had great stories. Unkind people would call them lies. When I was small he told me about one time he made a scarecrow. And the scarecrow was so effective that not alone did the crows not take any potatoes but they left back the ones they took the year before.
WILLIE,	That's a cod.
SEAN;	And he had another story about a cleeving straddle.. He was drawing out turf with an ass and cleeves.. Do you know the creels that you see on the backs of donkeys. You'd see them nowadays on postcards and such like? Well up in Rathea they're called "cleeves" and they're held in position by a "cleeving-straddle"; which is a saddle-like harness with a spike, or hook, on either side to hold the cleeves.
	Anyway the Salmon was using said mode of haulage when, due to inadequate upholstering, didn't he cleeving-straddle irritate and cut the ass, leaving a nasty lesion on either side of his backbone. (The ass's now, not the Salmon's)
	The weather being warm of course the flies attacked the open wounds, which festered (savin' your presence) developing into two raw nasty-looking holes in the ass's back.
	The ass, tired after a hard day's work, went out and lay down at the back of the house under a hawthorn tree. And what do you think but didn't a couple of haws fall into the holes in his back. The holes eventually healed but the next Spring didn't two little whitethorn trees sprout up out of his back.

Do you know what the Salmon did? (according to himself). He waited for them to grow fairly strong and then he sawed them off about four inches from the base. And thereafter he had the only ass in Ireland with a permanent cleeving-straddle.

(When Sean notices that Willie is not amused by his story he sits down on the stool and puts his head in his hands)

WILLIE;   Are you coming home or are you going to stay here?

SEAN: *(Standing up and moving slowly towards the right)* I'm doing neither. I've been thinking….. I left home yesterday to better myself and at the first sign of rejection I turned back. My people were mountainy people and they wouldn't be impressed. A mountainy person shouldn't turn back. *(He turns around and shakes hands with Willie)*

SEAN: Goodbye Willie. *(Sean exits) Willie, mesmerised, mumbles "goodbye", hesitates centre stage before exiting and Sean can be heard singing "Finuge".)*
There is a cabin by a glen,
The place where I was born.
There eagles fly the summer sky
To greet the smiling morn.
Finuge, Finuge, oh golden wood
You meadows wild…………..
(*Song fades out)*

CURTAIN.

SCENE THREE.

Time; 1980.

Set; a narrow boreen with a small bridge-wall running three-quarters the length of stage. It is Summer and wild flowers are in bloom at the end of the wall. There is a sound of water gurgling.

Sean McCarthy *(now in his mid-fifties)* is sitting on the low wall smoking a Meerschaum pipe. He is casually dressed in a good quality tweed jacket and twill trousers. He is writing in a copybook. A girl can be heard approaching singing a pop song.*(Maggie Sheehan enters. She is aged about fourteen or slightly more and is dressed in a school uniform. She is a lively, pleasant girl)*

MAGGIE:	Hello.
SEAN:	Hello girleen. You have a lovely voice. What's your name?
MAGGIE:	Maggie Sheehan.
SEAN:	Ah, your father was Tim Sheehan. He died young, may he have a bed in Heaven. He was a dancing teacher..... and a powerful singer. That's where you got the voice from; you didn't lick it off the ground.
MAGGIE:	My mother says I got it from her.
SEAN:	Yes, she was a Stack from Lyre. A talented family too you got it on the double. *(Pauses)* You don't know me.
MAGGIE:	I do so. You're Sean McCarthy, the songwriter.
SEAN:	That's right, but a young one like you wouldn't be interested in my songs.
MAGGIE,	Yes I would and Sister Ignatious asked me to sing one of your songs yesterday.
SEAN:	Which one?
Maggie:	" Where Wild Winds Blow".
SEAN:	And did you know the words of it?

MAGGIE: I did, I know the words of all you songs.
SEAN: Yerrah, no you don't. I wrote 160 songs. How would
            you know the words of them all?
MAGGIE: Which one do I not know?
SEAN: Eh....eh.... Cloheen.
            (*She sings "Cloheen"*)

I have seen the green fields of my native Cloheen,
I have walked in the valley by a rippling stream,
I've seen the proud eagle soar high in the sky.
I have cried o'er the grave where my Mary does lie.

These twenty five years I have sailed the seas wide,
I have watched golden sunsets with sadness my guide.
The memories haunt me, at night I do dream,
I still walk with my Mary along by Cloheen.

I can still see her standing where the bright waters flow,
And the Church where we married so long, long ago.
I welcome the morning it brings peace of mind,
From the dreams of the young love that I left behind.

The day of our marriage, we walked hand in hand.
No prouder man walked on this green fertile land.
No honeymoon bower, no baby to cry,
Just a quiet lonely grave, where my Mary does lie.

So adieu lovely Mary, rest well in Cloheen,
In your grave you've found peace by the rippling stream,
The proud eagle guard you from high in the sky,
And a rose marks the grave where my young love does lie.

SEAN: That song was born when an old man pointed a
            gnarled finger at a clump of briars and bushes to
            show me a famine grave. When I asked how many
            perished he looked dreamily at Knockanoir and said,
            " Only one, the rest took the cattle boat to America".

"You'll have no trouble finding it" he said. And I didn't. When I scraped the moss off a flat stone I could read the inscription, "MARY R.I.P." Then I wondered... Was she young?.....Was she beautiful?....Did she have a lover....? Did her eyes shine when she heard a young man singing in a moonlit meadow? I had no way of knowing. But I used my imagination to put her story in song. And some day your story will be told in song. And it will be a story of success. You'll go places girl. You have the voice, you have the personality and you have the confidence. *(As if to himself)* I sang songs, wrote songs and poems. I wrote stories. I even wrote a book but I didn't have the confidence. The world didn't succeed in taking Sands's bog out of me. Whether I was in Fort Sade or Philadelphia I always perceived myself as a Kerry bogman, who couldn't spell, typed with one finger and had no idea where commas went. But that's another story.

Maggie;   You have plenty of other stories but I have to be going, bye.

SEAN;   o nEirigh an Bhotair leat.

(He sits down, takes a battered school-copy from his pockets and thoughtfully peruses it)

SEAN: I took a bit of poetic licence with that one. Killury's Golden Corn. Sure Killury wouldn't feed a snipe not to mind grow corn. As John Joe Kennelly said about Killocrim, "..... if the land was any poorer the crows would have to carry flasks". But nobody lives in Killury so I won't have any objections from the natives.....but the song......*(closes eyes and sits back)* I can hear it....I can hear that young Sheehan one singing it. *Sean hears Maggie singing Killury's Golden Corn in his head.")* (*"*

Where are you now Sean Hanrahan
In that cold land far away.
Can you not hear the wild birds call
In the hills across the bay.
The cooing winds are blowing love,
As in the days of yore
And the wild winds keep a rolling
On the lonely Kerry Shore.

The soft dew is falling love
Upon the Mountain side.
The meadows green near Beencuneen
Keep singing to the tide.
The piper plays his lonely air
To greet the smiling morn'
And the summer rain keeps falling
On Killury's Golden Corn.

The prison yard is dark and bare
Where no man speaks my name.
Van Dieman's peak though sad and bleak,
Can't hide my burning shame.
My eyes grow dim remembering
The love that once I knew
And a smiling maid that loved me there
Where falls the morning dew.

Sometimes I dream of my Maura Lee
Though it was long ago.
I hear the wild birds singing free
In the valley down below.
I see you smiling in the sun
To kiss the summer dawn
And the soft rain that keeps falling
On Killury's Golden Corn.

The famine walls and mountains tall
That took my youth from me
The cold–eyed stranger came to take
Me o'r the raging sea.
They stole the sunlight from my eyes
And the love my soul did know
And I left you waiting Maura Lee
Where the soft winds gently blow.

Once I walked my broken land
To light the burning flame
Through fields and glens we wandered then
To play the freedom games
Some died in lanes with twisted limbs
Where wild flowers sweetly bloom.
Their young eyes closed forever now
To a weeping harvest moon.

My span of life is over
And peace steals over me
My soul will fly that stormy sky,
Across the raging sea.
Place me near my Maura Lee
n the land where I was born,
Then I'll hear the soft rain falling
On Killury's Golden Corn.

CURTAIN

SCENE FOUR.

Set; The same as scene three. It is now winter and the
vegetation at the end of the bridge wall are dead.
Time 1981 (about eighteen months after scene one).
Sean McCarthy is fishing. He is dressed in a wax-
jacket and a Fly-decked hat.
He has a cane rod and is casting across "the fourth
wall", facing the audience. Maggie Sheehan enters
from L. She has matured and is now wearing makeup,
lipstick and high heels. She sneaks up behind Sean
and sings the opening line of "John O ' Halloran".

SEAN: Mother o' God you frightened the life out of me.
             And worse than that you're after frightening the fish.
             These Smearla trout are elusive hoors at the best of
             times...that song you're singing..... that was judged
             the Best Contemporary People's Song by the English
             Song and Dance Society.....and....yet.....women didn't
             like it.

MAGGIE: But I'm different. How did you come to write it? Is
             there a true story behind it?

SEAN: There is. (*He sits on the wall*) I met an 81 year-old,
             toil-worn Irishman one night in Camden Town. It
             turned out that he was John O 'Halloran who had
             left Tralee sixty years before to make his fortune
             in England. We got talking and his story was an
             interesting one. I went back to The Mother Redcap
             every night for five weeks. Although God knows, at
             the time, I didn't need much encouragement. I sat
             with him night after night listening to his tales of
             love, of disappointment, of fighting, working and
             hardship.Then one night John O 'Halloran was
             missing....
             I found out from the Irish lads that he had died in his
             lonely bed the previous night.
             After a lifetime of toil across the length and breadth

48

of England he left tuppence ha'penny and a Scapular Medal.

A couple of days later, as the noise of the London traffic reverberated on the tombstones we buried John O'Halloran. There were only four of us. The Priest, myself and two others.....I went back to my own digs and wrote "John O 'Halloran".

And now that you have frightened my fish you may as well sing it for me.

(Maggie sings "John O 'Halloran")

My name is John O 'Halloran, and I'm eighty-one years old.
I left my boyhood days behind, for to search for fame and gold.
I left my home in Tralee town, in my twenty-second year.
I would dig the gold on England's shore, and I'd make my fortune there.

The weary months in search of work, the tramp through street and road,
A shake-me-down in Camden Town, it was my first abode.
No friendly glance to cheer my heart, no man to shake my hand,
No easy gold only rain and cold, in this God Forsaken land.

Go down that trench Proud Irishman, for you are strong and big,
Go take that shovel by the neck, spit on your hands and dig.
Tear out the guts from Mother Earth, from the dawn till fading light,
In the nearest pub you'll spend your sub, and you'll hate and love and fight.

I have tramped around this country now, for fifty years or more,
I've met some women in my time, the good one and the whore.
I've tramped it down to Preston town, I have skippered in the rain,
I've cursed and prayed, I've been poorly paid,
I've known hunger, joy and pain.

I loved a girl in Liverpool, a sweet one from Mayo,

I've slept with girls from Tiger Bay, with teeth like virgin snow.
I have ate my foods in small sheebeens, and I've drunk the porter black,
A dirty bed for to lay my head, where the lice crawled up my back.

My bones are getting weary now, and my shoulders they are bent,
My once black hair is grey with care and my money is all spent.
Soon Sargent Death will call me home, and he'll take me by the hand,
Far from Tralee Town, lay my body down, in this God forsaken land.
To all the men who dig it out, adieu my friends, adieu,
To young and old, in search of gold, I raise my glass to you.
Go down that trench Proud Irishman, take the shovel in your hand,
There's no easy gold only rain and cold, in this God forsaken land.

MAGGIE: It's certainly not a jolly song.

SEAN: It's a brutal song. Very few of my songs are jolly. And yet I suppose I expect other people to write funny songs. I once asked Ewen McColl," Why is there no humour in any of your songs"?
He must have been trying to beat a Kerryman at his own game because he answered with a question. He said, " Why does somebody have to die in all your songs"?

MAGGIE: And he was right.

SEAN: I suppose he was.I was always moved to write by death but I was inspired by other things as well.
I remember one winter in London the frost was so bad that all construction work was at a standstill. You'd see fellows "breaking" their Donkey-jackets in the morning before they could put them on.
At the time I was employed by an English pub-landlord, six nights a week, to sing ballads. Of course with no building work there was no money. And that meant there was nobody to listen to my

rebel-songs. So I was out of a job until the weather improved. One evening I was lying on my cold, rickety, bed reading a dog-eared Reader's Digest when I came across an article by a writer called Ernest Deeling. The story was headed, "Captain Brady and his Highland Paddys".
I read it carefully and promised myself that when times got better I'd travel to Kilkenny and get the full story. Things did improve and the next year I went to Kilkenny. I met a hard-drinking, white-haired historian by the name of Daniel Keegan.
Between songs, political arguments and fishing lies Daniel told me the story and I composed a so........

MAGGIE, Yes, I know. You wrote "Highland Paddy".
(She sings "Highland Paddy")

One evening fair as the sun was shining,
To Kilkenny I did ride,
I did meet with Captain Brady -
A tall commander by his side.

Chorus:
Then you are welcome Highland Paddy,
By my side you'll surely stand, hear the people shout for freedom,
We'll rise in the morning with the Fenian band,
Rise in the morning with the Fenian band.

In the mornin' we rose early
Just before the break of dawn blackbirds singing in the bushes
Greetings to a smiling morn.
Gather round me men of Ireland
Gather Fenians gather round
Hand to hand with sword and musket
Spill the blood upon this holy ground.
There's a glen beside the river

Just outside Kilkenny Town
There we met this noble captain
Men lay dead upon the ground.
Chorus
There's a grave beside the river
A mile outside Kilkenny Town
There we laid our noble captain
Birds were silent when this Fenian died
All my life I will remember
I'll remember night and day
That once I rode into Kilkenny
And I heard this noble captain say.
Chorus

SEAN: I always had great faith in the ballad as the keeper of our heritage. I remember James Connolly's daughter saying, ".....more may be remembered of a country's history and treasured deep in the heart of people through a song or a poem than through the pages of a history book".

MAGGIE: Will you feck off, you and your history. Listen.....I was asked the other day how you came to write "Fair Sinead" and I didn't know. Was she a great love in your life?

SEAN: She was, but not in the way you might think. A few years ago, above in Dublin, I was singing with a Folk-group called "The Weavers". and one day I called to see young Warfield of The Wolfe Tones. His beautiful blue-eyed baby daughter, Sinead, was in her cot playing with a big brown Teddy-bear. I don't know what she thought of the mumbling Kerryman with the hat looking down at her but I went into my brother Mick's pub, The Embankment, in Tallagh and I wrote "My Blue-eyed Fair Sinead" at the counter. I felt compelled to write that song. But then....I always did have a weakness for blue-eyed beauties.

MAGGIE: *(Pretending to be hurt)* And I thought you might
have written it for me

SEAN: As it turns out, I wrote them all for you. *(He gestures
towards centre stage. She sings "Fair Sinead")*
Last night I heard an angel cry sweet dreams did
haunt my sleep,
I dreamt of valleys decked with flowers and wild
streams running deep.
And then I heard from far away a moonlight
serenade,
It was my young love calling me, the blue-eyedFair
Sinead.

There all in the silent room my treasure she did smile
Like Helen fair beyond compare she does my heart
beguile.
Golden sunlight in her hair, my lovely Irish maid
I hold the wide world in my arms the blue-eyed Fair
Sinead.

Some men travel far and wide great wonders for to
see
The ravaged lands of "Samarkand" or the shores of
Galilee.
Others strive for the yellow gold for ivory and jade
But Kings and Queens do envy me the blue-eyed Fair
Sinead.

What fairy wind did bring you here to shine your love
on me
What Guardian Angel from above was watching
carefully.
Beside you diamonds will not shine, the brightest jew-
els do fade,
The stars at night do hide their light for my blue-eyed
Fair Sinead.

> Now close your eyes my lovely one your tiny hand in mine
> I will guard my baby girl until the morning time
> Peace be on your pillow love, rest well in tender shade
> The new born day is breaking soon for my blue-eyed Fair Sinead.
> (*Maggie sits down on the wall*)

SEAN;	Looking at the pendant she is wearing) What's that?
MAGGIE,	It's a medal.
SEAN:	I know it's a medal. What sort of a medal?
MAGGIE,	An All-Ireland medal.
SEAN;	Listen girl, I don't have much of an interest in sport but I've seen enough All-Ireland medals in North Kerry to know that's not one...you wouldn't see Eddie Walshe or Joe Keohane with anything like that. An All-Ireland medal has a football on it and four......
MAGGIE:	(*Feigning impatience*) It's a Comhaltas medal. I won the All-Ireland at the Fleadh.
SEAN:	Well good girl. What song did you sing?
MAGGIE,	"Lough Sheelin's Side."
SEAN:	A lovely song; (*Sings*).

> Farewell my country a long farewell.
> My tale of anguish no tongue can tell.
> For I'm forced to fly o'er the ocean wide
> From the home I loved by Lough Sheelin's side.

SEAN;	A sad song....like my own songs.
MAGGIE:	It's not as sad as your songs. Nothing is as sad as your songs.
SEAN,	(*Dreamily*) Maybe someday you'd sing one of my sad songs in an All-Ireland Final.
MAGGIE:	I might.
SEAN:	What song would you sing?

MAGGIE;   What song would I sing? What song would I sing?
SEAN;   Sure you have plenty of time to decide. I'll be going.
             Bye. *(He exits right)*
Maggie;   *(Absent-mindedly)* Goodbye Sean.
             *(Suddenly she jumps up and sings "The Beating Of
             The Drum)*

O run my lovely Nora the time is near at hand,
A thousand men are on parade awaiting the command.
There is handsome Johnny, a shouldering his gun
There standing to attention to the beating of the drum.

Chorus;
Hark, hark the drums are beating love no longer can I stay
I hear a bugle calling, a call I must obey.
I must get my rifle and march for many a mile
And fight the German soldiers on the banks of the Nile.

Oh, Johnny dearest Johnny don't leave me here to die
My father has disowned me for the bearing of our boy.
Do not use your rifle, love, to take another's life
Stay at home lovely Johnny and make me your wife.

Oh, Darling lovely Nora, you knew the time would come
That I would go a-marching to the beating of the drum
The Queen has sent her orders to come and meet the foe.
To the desert lands of Egypt your Johnny he must go.

Chorus;
Hear the trumpet sounding now across the barrack square
I can see the sunlight a-shining on your hair.
Wave to me fair Nora the march it has begun
The blowing of the bugle and the beating of the drum.

The war is all over and the ship is sailing in
Happy wives are waiting to greet the fighting men.
Hear the bugle, Nora, just stay a little while,

Your Johnny he lies buried on the banks of the Nile.
Chorus.

SEAN: (*Entering from Right*) I forgot me bloody fishing rod..
MAGGIE: 'Good enough for you when you wouldn't wait to
                    listen to me.
SEAN: I was listening. That song is the story of a 17-year
                    old Wicklow boy who died by a German bullet. The
                    German bullet couldn't tell the difference between
                    Aldershot and Aughavanagh. Johnny represents
                    every young man who listened to John Redmond and
                    his likes telling them that they were going to fight
                    for the freedom of small nations. And Kitchener (a
                    Kerryman, I'm sorry to say) and his "your country
                    needs you".I was conscripted into the British Army
                    during the Second World War you know. I was a
                    reluctant soldier and I didn't see one angry German
                    but I wrote a song for the British army called "
                    Rudolph Hess". It was sung all over the Middle East.
                    But I'll tell you about that next week.
MAGGIE: You won't see me next week ......unless you come to
                    Dublin
SEAN: I won't see yo.....?
MAGGIE,   I'm going to live in Dublin. I'm going to be a nurse.
SEAN: Well, I'll miss you. And may God look after you and
                    bless your work. I know you won't lose the run of
                    yourself. And I know you won't lose your Rathea
                    accent. My people came from Rathea. And while
                    I'm no Nostradamus or Colmcille I can predict that
                    you'll come back to Kerry and I know that when
                    you marry you'll marry for love. You know Maggie,
                    not everyone marries for love. I wrote a poem about
                    someone who didn't. Will I read it for you?
MAGGIE: I suppose you will.
                    (*He takes a sheet of paper from his pocket and reads
                    Darling Kate*)

You are fair of face, dear Kate, now you're nearing twenty-one,
I hesitate to spoil your dreams, when your life has just begun.
Your father, he is old, a grah, and I am far from strong,
A dowry from John Hogan's son would help us all along.

Just think of it, my darling Kate, you would own a motor car,
You'd wear fine linen next your skin and travel near and far.
Hogan's lands stretch far and wide, from Rathea to Drummahead;
He owns sheep and cows and fine fat sows; pyjamas for the bed.

I know he's tall and skinny, Kate, and his looks are not the best,
But beggars can't be choosers, love, when you're feathering your nest!
He's been to college in the town; his shirts are always new,
What does it matter if he's old, he's just the man for you.

I know you love young Paddy Joe, him with the rakish eye,
I've seen the way you look at him whenever he goes by.
I will admit he's handsome, Kate, but he doesn't own a car,
Sure, he likes to fight and drink all night above in Sheehan's bar.

Did I ever tell you, Kate a grah... that I was pretty too?
The summer days seemed longer then, and the sky was always blue!
I was only gone nineteen, and your father fifty-three,
But he owned the land on which we stand and he seemed the man for me.

There was a young man lived next door, I loved with all my might,
It was his face that haunted me when your father held me tight;
I longed, dear Kate, down through the years, for the soft touch of his hand.
But young love is no substitute for ten acres of fine land.

You will wear a long white dress and a red rose in your hair,

I will throw confetti, Kate, the whole town will be there;
You will make a promise true, to honour and obey,
I will stand on your right hand, and I'll sell my love away.

Tears are not for daytime, Kate, but only for the night,
You'll have a daughter of your own and teach her wrong from right;
Rear her strong and healthy, Kate, pray guidance from above.
Then one fine day when she's nineteen—she might marry just for love.

SEAN;	What do you think of that?
MAGGIE:	It's a sorrowful tale of greed, frustration, insecurity....and hope, told as only you can tell it.
SEAN:	Thank you. Do you know that some people think that poem is funny and that they're meant to laugh at it. I didn't write many monologues. The songs went well for me. But it was a long haul. Songwriting is a long haul. But it worked out fairly well. (*Looking into the middle-distance*) Few things would give me more pleasure than to hear your voice coming out of a Juke-box in Tralee, or London or New York or South Carolina......will you record my songs?
MAGGIE:	(*Playfully*) Sean McCarthy, I have better things to be doing than recording your oul songs.
SEAN,	Better things to be doin....? What better things?
MAGGIE:	(*Skipping away*) Aah, that would be telling you.

CURTAIN

SCENE FIVE..

Time; 1990. .
Set; A sparsely furnished living room. There are books, notebooks and newspapers scattered around. There is a large picture of the Clancy Brothers and Tommy Makem, a rosary Beads and a calendar for 1990 on the wall.

Sean (*Now in his mid sixties*) is sitting in an armchair writing in a journal. There is a knock at the door).

SEAN,   (*Without looking up*) Come in.
(*Maggie enters. She is now in her mid twenties and casually dressed*)

SEAN: (*Surprised jumps up and hugs her*) Maggie. I heard you were back. How are you?

MAGGIE: I'm all right. I'm an oul married woman now.

SEAN,   Did I ever tell you what my uncle the Tumbler McCarthy had to say about marriage (I didn't agree with him, mind you)? He told me; " ….. a woman is different from a greyhound. When a greyhound can't chase the hare anymore he can sit by the fire. But once a female has you fettered to a piece of Holy Paper she'll sit by the fire and nag you day and night". And another of his spakes was; " What's good for the Nanny is good for the Puck providing they don't lock horns".

MAGGIE: It seems the Tumbler had many profound statements about the nuptial state. Are you sure you didn't agree with him?

SEAN: I didn't. Sure I got married…..Sure enough I was 48 at the time. Herself and myself spend a lot of our time on opposite sides of the Atlantic. So, I'm a happily married bachelor. (*Pause*) I knew you'd come back Maggie. I travelled the world but the bog was always calling. You see Maggie, people like you and me, we can't ever leave, our hearts are rooted here. Someone once asked James Joyce if he would ever return to Dublin and he said, "Did I ever leave?"

SEAN;   (*Awkwardly, after a pause*) I'm sure you didn't sing any of my songs in Dublin.

MAGGIE: I did so. I won a competition in Rathmines with one of your songs.

SEAN: Good girl, keep winning.

MAGGIE: That reminds me. When I won the All-Ireland you said something to me about "winners" but I was young and I'm afraid I wasn't listening. Do you remember what it was?

SEAN: I do. I was quoting a Greek historian; Polly Bus, or something like that was his name. He said, " Those who know how to win are more numerous than those who know how to make proper use of their victory". But that doesn't apply to you, my love.....wh....what was the song?

MAGGIE: In Shame Love In Shame.

SEAN: Ah. That's a special song. As the poet Shelley said, "The sweetest songs are those that tell the saddest tale".That song was my Salvation. My sister, Peggy McCarthy, the light o' Heaven to her, died on Sunday 10th February 1946.

She got pregnant out of wedlock and became the victim of the times, of gossip and of the so-called moral values of the day.

She was refused admission to three hospitals in north Kerry and she died giving birth on the side of the road. And then, in Death, the gates of Listowel Church were closed against her coffin.

I harboured hatred and resentment for years. Until, I suppose you could say, I became a child again. I told my old schoolmaster about it. "Write about the bloody thing" says he. And I did.....to try and get the hatred out of my system and unsnarl my gut.

The hatred grew less and less each day after I wrote

"In Shame Love In Shame". I owe a lot to that song
and I haven't heard it sung for years.

MAGGIE;   I'll sing it now....and sing it well (nudges him) just to
show that I know how to, "make proper use of my
victory".

(She sings "In Shame Love In Shame")

They whisper their stories
And they glance with the eye.
They look over my shoulder when I pass them by.
My father and mother they treat me the same,
Hear the nightingale crying in shame love in shame.

Oh cling to me tight love, take hold of my hand.
The road it is long love and harsh is the land.
That's the cross we must carry, for having no name,
Hear the nightingale crying in shame love in shame.

I had wings to my feet and of love I have dreamed,
The moon and the stars how friendly they seemed.
The touch of his hand, in the soft summer rain,
Hear the nightingale crying in shame love in shame.

Oh! Once in the starlight when he held me close,
Down by the green meadow, where grew the wild rose.
The wind sang of love, Oh! How soft it's refrain,
But the nightingale cries now, in shame love in shame.

Now hush little darling, we soon will be there,
A blanket of love, will surround you with care.
No vile tongues will whisper, you will never feel pain.
Hear the nightingale crying in shame love in shame.

The meek will inherit, I have heard this decree,
And suffer small children to come unto me.
The sins of the father on your head will be lain,
Hear the nightingale crying in shame love in shame.

How mute are the birds now, my bonny young boy.
How deep is the river, how silent your cry.
The waters baptise you, then we'll both have a name.
Hear the nightingale sing there's no shame, there's no shame.
(As the song finishes Sean is staring at the ground)

MAGGIE;   What are you day-dreaming about now?
SEAN;   I was thinking about how some songs come about.
               I remember once on a fair-day in Kanturk, County
               Cork, when I heard children with a skipping rhyme.
               And many years later I was on a building site in
               London, hiding under a concrete stairs from the
               foreman, when I wrote a song around that skipping
               rhyme. And I was just thinking that if Murphy's
               foreman had been a bit more vigilant we wouldn't
               have that particular song.
               It spent twenty-six weeks in the top twenty sung
               by Danny Doyle, a young Dublinman. It has been
               recorded by dozens of singers around the world and it
               must have been sung a million times.
MAGGIE: Make that a million and one. *(She sings "Step It Out*
               Mary".)

In the village of Kilgory, there's a maiden young and fair
Her eyes they shine like diamonds, she has long and golden hair
But the countryman comes riding, rides up to her father's gates
Riding on a milk-white stallion, he comes at the strike of eight.
Chorus:
Step it out, Mary, my fine daughter
Step it out, Mary, if you can
Step it out, Mary, my fine daughter
Show your legs to the countryman.

I have come to court your daughter, Mary of the golden hair
I have gold and I have silver, I have goods beyond compare
I will buy her silks and satin and a gold ring for her hand,
I will buy for her a mansion, she'll have servants to command

I don't want your gold and silver, I don't want your house and land
I am going with a soldier, I have promised him my hand
But the father spoke up sharply: You will do as you are told,
You'll get married on the Sunday and you'll wear that ring of gold.

In the village of Kilgory there's a deep stream flowing by
On her marriage day at midnight she drowned with her soldier boy
In the cottage there is music, you can hear her father say:
Step it out, Mary, my fine daughter, Sunday is your wedding day.

SEAN;   I wrote that song on a piece of a cement bag and I
           always regretted not keeping the original manuscript.
MAGGIE;   As concrete proof like? What are you working on
           now?
SEAN;   I'm writing a piece for "The Kerryman". About
           two years ago they commissioned me to write 100
           weekly articles titled "McCarthy's Women" in which
           I would profile a different woman each week. Well,
           I was in Tralee yesterday; (I had to go to the hospital
           for a bit of an oul test), I was talking to the Editor
           and he said, "Sean, you're after doin' ninety-nine
           women......."
MAGGIE;   WHAT???
SEAN;   The Editor told me that I have profiled ninety-nine
           women to date. "You have one to go, Sean" says he,
           "Who is it going to be?" I didn't tell him. I just said,
           "This last one is my favourite". And so she is.
MAGGIE;   Who is it?
SEAN;   Ah, that would be telling you.

CURTAIN

SCENE SIX.

Set; The same as in Scene five but the papers and books have been tidied up somewhat. "The Kerryman" is lying on a coffee table.
(There is a knock on the door and Maggie enters R.) She is wet, wearing a raincoat and carrying an umbrella)

MAGGIE;   Hello.

SEAN;   (From bedroom) I'll be with you in a minute. I was having a bit of a lie down.

MAGGIE   (Spotting "The Kerryman" she takes it up and starts to read;) "Mc Carthy's Women..... The last in the series......by Sean McCarthy.....Maggie Sheehan..... bright future as a folksinger....voice like a nightingale in Renagown......she loves roses.....but hates ironing......she comes from a ......"
(Sean enters from L. He is dressed in shirt and trousers and in his stockinged feet).

MAGGIE;   You were looking for me.

SEAN;   I want you to sing a song.

MAGGIE;   You brought me out on a night like that because you want me "to sing a song".

SEAN;   There's something else as well.

MAGGIE;   Well, I hope it's good. You're after taking me away from my housework (indicating "The Kerryman") even if I don't like ironing.

Sean;   Will you record my songs before I die?

MAGGIE;   I don't know the air of that one........yes I'll record your songs....sometime.

SEAN;   Will you do it soon?

MAGGIE;   We'll see.....what do you want me to sing now?

SEAN;   Dan Malone.

    (She Sings "Dan Malone")

Oh, me name is Dan Malone
I've no place to call me home.
I'm an outcast in the land that I was born in.
And I'm weary of the load
On this long and lonely road.
How I hate to face the sunlight in the morning.

Oh the land is rich and wide
But hunger walks beside.
I'm an outcast in this proud land that bore me.
My life is almost done
And my courage is all gone
For the long road that stretches out before me.

Then that day so long ago
I met Kitty from Mayo.
Fair of face, her voice forever charmed me.
But she couldn't bear the load
On this long and lonely road.
Now her grave lies on a hill outside Killarney.

I have begged from time to time.
I have drunk the golden wine.
I've fought men and I've done my share of lovin'.
I've met wise men; I've met fools.
But we've always known the rules.
A tinker man must always be a movin'.

Ah but maybe one day soon
When the heather is in bloom,
I lay my head upon the scented clover.
A man can't always fight,
And so a long winter's night
I'll go to sleep; my troubles will be over.

Then remember Dan Malone
As I lie here all alone

Remember me to this proud land that bore me.
I can sleep my time away
In six feet of pauper's clay,
No open road lay stretching out before me.

SEAN;   " I can sleep my life away, in six feet of pauper's clay,
         No open road lay stretching out before me".
         Poor Dan Malone. He knew every blade of grass
         from Dunfanaghy to Valentia Island. He told me
         his life story one day at a Fleadh in Listowel. It
         was shortly before he went for the big sleep. I think
         he was about seventy. I'm three years short of the
         Biblical span. But I did a fair bit of living. I'm sure I
         squeezed it in.

MAGGIE; You devoted the first half of your life to writing about
         death, are you going to spend the rest of it talking
         about it?
         Why don't you write a song about living, like "Sweet
         Rathcoole".

(She starts to sing "Sweet Rathcoole").

It was up in sweet Rathcoole, one fine bright day in June,
That I first met Katie Conroy when the wild flowers were in bloom.
"Bedad meself" says I "'Tis a shameful thing to see
Such a fine big strappin' girl with no man upon her knee.

SEAN;   *(interrupting her and handing her an envelope)* I
         want you to learn this song....as soon as you can.
         It's called "My Kerry Hill". A lot of my songs were
         shallow; they lacked dept.
         But in this, my last song, I have endeavoured to
         capture it all. The hopes of youth, the pride of
         ancestry, the fire of patriotism and hopefully the
         resignation of the dyi............will you promise me
         that you'll record my songs?

MAGGIE;   Have I ever let you down before?
SEAN;   No. When will you record them?
MAGGIE;   I dunno. Some year or other.*(Seeing the
           disappointment on his face)* ah I'm only joking
           you. As a matter of fact I have booked a studio
           in Killarney for two days next week to record
           (She gestures theatrically) "The Songs Of Sean
           McCarthy".
SEAN;   Thank God for that.
MAGGIE;   *(Exiting R.)* and now I must be getting back to my
           ironing. It's not a night for roses.
SEAN;   God be with you.
 SEAN;   *(Addressing the picture of the Clancy Brothers and
           Tommy Makem)* I couldn't tell her......I didn't have
           the heart. ....How could I tell a person as caring as
           her......How would I say, "Maggie, I got the results
           of the tests. I've been diagnosed with cancer.....I have
           three months to live".
           But, with the help of God I'll survive to hear her sing
           my songs on the radio. *(He sits down and he can
           hear Maggie singing " My Kerry Hill" to musical
           accompaniment)*

The night is long love, the hours grow weary,
Youthful memories soon fade away.
A voice keeps calling from days of yore, love
Magic moments of yesterday.
Do you remember Sweet September,
Young love searching for a golden thrill.
And the days were merry
When we plucked wild berries,
On the verdant slopes of a Kerry Hill.

The time is fleeting, the new moon peeping,
Stars are dancing with heel and toe.
An old man's story recounts the glory
Of the brave deeds of long ago.

Children listen with eyes that glisten,
Fish jump high in a mountain rill.
Lovers walking and softly talking
All alone on a Kerry Hill.

I often wonder where are my school friends,
Some have gone far across the sea,
And some are weeping or in the Church-yard sleeping
Lying safe where the wind blows free,
Can they hear the banshee wailing,
In the moon-light soft and still
Or hear a piper softly playing
Forgotten airs on a Kerry Hill.

I often dream nights of fairest Nora,
I hear her voice in the Summer air,
I see her green eyes filled with love light
Moon beams shading her golden hair.
I walked the green land by the meadow
Near the long, long silent mill,
To place a wild rose on a green grave
Where she lies on a Kerry Hill.

  And I remember the green hills burning
When the strangers with cold eyes came,
Maidens sighing and young men dying,
Like wild flowers crushed in the Summer rain.
Then the bells of freedom chiming.
A moon-lit meadow where young men drill
A green flag flowing, a trumpet blowing
Loud and clear on a Kerry Hill.

(Sean stands up, takes a Rosary beads from the wall and exits L. singing the last verse himself)

I must away now from the green groves
My time of talking is surely done,
My bones are weary from life's long journey
My time of being is nearly gone.
To hear again the pipers playing
In the moon-light soft and still
No more grieving I am a-leaving
To say goodbye to my Kerry Hill.

CURTAIN.

© Mattie Lennon 2006

THE PERFECT PASSENGER

Mark Bolger

Now for those of us out there in the trenches the idea of the perfect passenger seems more myth than reality. Is there such a thing? Do they exist? Or are they just the wishful thinking of a bored driver trying to tune out whilst stuck in George's Street, with what seems like an Einstein/Hawkins type paradox of infinite traffic existing on finite streets.

So to unearth this intangible character there are a few things that need to be addressed. So, is the perfect passenger a matter of perception, will my perfect passenger be another drivers nightmare. Now I suppose there is the possibility that there is one single type that would be viewed universally as perfect, that quintessential traveller who would be viewed by all my colleagues as the holy-grail to be sought out and cherished when found. However just like those in question, drivers also come in many shapes and sizes, although it seems from my personal observation that drivers past a certain level of service all seem to assume the same shape, evolution at work or something else? I don't know, you answer, but the day I look down and have a groove in my stomach that I can neatly slot the steering wheel into is the day that I rethink my career choice.

Having such a range of personalities and cultures driving buses in the city today makes finding the one category of passenger that would appease everyone all the more elusive. Consequently what we need to do is eliminate those that are unanimously disliked. In order to do this particular list justice I would probably need more pages than the editor would allow, accordingly I'll list the usual suspects, the Top Five most Unwanted if you will. Top of the list for me has to go with those lovely citizens who while standing at the stop, watch Dublin traffic grind to a halt for yet another peak time, even as they watch you achingly make your way to their stop in little five foot increments, and when you finally get to the stop to do your duty as the conscientious professionals we all are, they see fit to start screaming at you about the fact that they have been waiting for over half an hour for a bus. Rather than point out the obvious, I've always found that treating them like kids (that they are doing a remarkably good impression of) and apologising and reassuring them that it will be all better tomorrow, normally makes them shut up and leave you alone. Watching them then sit stewing in their own ire is enough to put the smile momentarily back on my face.

A close second is those mothers who know... Before I get into this, don't hate me because I'm having a go at mothers, I have one myself. Anyway those mothers who know they are getting on a bus and decide to wait until you pull up to the stop before they decide to take their shopping off the pram handles, pull poor little Tommy aggressively out of his seat, then try to watch that he doesn't step onto the road while trying to fold the pram with about as much success and grace as a chimp doing a Rubik's cube, all the while glancing daggers at the driver as if he's the reason that she now feels pressured and flustered. When the colossal task (sarcasm) of having the buggy and shopping in one hand and pushing the child up the steps with the other is finished, she then proceeds to dig her purse out which wouldn't you know, is at the bottom of her shopping, telling little Tommy to go sit down and then when he independently trots off to do just that yelling at him to come back. And when you think it just could not get any worse the fare proceeds to be counted out in coppers, and you get that silly little "I'm sorry for holding you up" grimace. Four minutes have passed.

A little footnote is that I'm not talking about mothers with new babies; I have some compassion after all.

Next up are the ever-present drunks; no matter what time of day, this particular species of Residentus Dublinis seems to favour public transport. Morning, noon or evening they stagger up the steps of your nice clean bus missing the occasional one, which then gets punctuated by some unintelligible growl that you can only guess is them unsuccessfully cursing at their feet, or wondering why the driver keeps moving the bus back and forth. They then try to root out the appropriate fare. One of these days I'm going to put my hand in one of their pockets, because I could swear they seem about two foot deep, their arms invariably go right in up to the elbow. Maybe all drunks should now be referred to as Dr. Whos, because their trousers are like the Tardis. Then with ninety proof breath they ask you to get the fare, at least I think that's what they ask because it's always followed by them sticking a nicotine stained hand full of change under your nose, managing to send one or two of the coins skittering down the bus in the process. So holding your breath just in case you are stopped and breathalysed, his exhalations alone are bound to fail you, you take his fare and then have to listen to a tirade of drunken mumblings peppered with 'bud' and 'brother'. Then he reaches in and slaps you on the shoulder, puts his thumb up and staggers toward a seat in a fog of alcohol fumes, hitting every bar in the bus on the way.

The last second smoker is next. This is the person who on seeing their bus approaching rather than accept fate and throw away the stub, frantically suck and suck, trying to dredge every last bit of kick from their habit. Getting on the bus might well be the last chance ever of getting a nicotine fix. With lungs filled to bursting with heavenly carcinogens they hold on to it like it's the last breath they'll ever take – that is until they ask for their fare and proceed to exhale every bit of that unhealthy cloud right in your face, oblivious to the strange fact that the driver has just turned green.

Last but not least is the person who sticks out their hand and as you get to the stop they realise that they had been a little bit hasty and yours is not the route they want. Rather than wave you on they turn to one side and completely ignore you, even when you do stop and open the doors they stare straight ahead absolutely refusing to make eye contact with you. If you call out and ask them if they want this particular route, they act completely oblivious to the fact that you have just spoken. All you can do is hope that when their bus does come along it will be full, and maybe, just maybe, the driver of the full bus will have a little sadistic streak and slow down until that crucial moment when they get their pass or money out, and then speed up again leaving the ignorer in a cloud of diesel fumes.

To add to those easily categorised five examples, are the people who regardless of the fact that there are signs on every bus cannot seem to remember to ring the bell when they want to get off. The lovely old dears who see fit to tell you where they are going, why they are going there and what particular ailment seems to be troubling them that week. The person who throws money into the money safe and then look at you while you try to do an impression of Uri Geller and psychically guess what they want. And of course the deep sea divers, or shareholders as they seem to love calling themselves, cackling at that, worn, used up joke with a gusto that is more fitting around a cauldron than on the steps of a double-decker bus.

Having dismissed all the obvious runners up in our search it seems to me that there is no one left to bestow the title 'The Perfect Passenger' on. Have I missed anyone? Or am I just being a cynic. No, I can't believe that about myself. 'Cynic' is a word coined by optimists to describe realists. That's what I think I am, a realist.

I wonder if it has always been like this, from that first entrepreneur who realised that letting people ride on his horse and cart for a small fee, to the complex system of transport that all urban areas need just to function today. Have passengers always been the colourful bunch that we deal with daily? After all this cogitation the one thing I can say with conviction is that, for myself, the perfect passenger is, the one who is travelling on any route except my own.

Unknown irishman changed the history of the world

John Cassidy

In 1789 France was in turmoil, the populace seething with discontent, the world of the nobility was about to collapse. The French revolution was about to change the future of France, of Europe and the Western world. On the 14th July, an Irish shoe maker named Seosamh Kavanagh and two companions started a rumour that soldiers of the King were about to attack the citizens of Paris.

He drove around the city in a horse and coach shouting "To the Bastille," " Capture the Bastille." With the mob behind him he went to the Hotel des Invalides, looted 30,000 muskets and led an assault on the Bastille. After four hours the Bastille, the symbol of all that the general population hated, fell. The French revolution had begun. There were thousands of Irish people and people of Irish descent in Paris and elsewhere in France in the 18th century. It was a natural place for refugees to go because contacts with France and Spain had been strong for generations. A hundred years previously 14,000 troops had to leave the country after the treaty of Limerick. " Flight of the Wild Geese."

All that remained of the old Irish Nobility and the middle classes fled to France, Spain and Austria along with ordinary Irish people, farmers and labourers. On the Continent the Irish joined armies, went into commerce and few were able to return home.

The French revolution influenced the affairs of Ireland. It had a great influence on the United Irishmen in the North of Ireland and contributed to the Rising there in 1798. It was indirectly a factor in the Wexford and Robert Emmett Rising in 1803. It also influenced the political and social life of the Country because of the effect it had on one man; Danial O'Connell.

The O'Connell's as Irish speaking people, had many connections with the Continent, many of the family living there, most educated there. Daniel O'Connell lived in Paris from 1791 until 1793 and was appalled by the terror, by the guillotining of the French nobility and many families with Irish associations.

The terror to which O'Connell reacted had as one of its leaders a man with interesting links to Ireland; Robespierre. Robespierre's ancestors had been expelled from Kilkenny by Cromwell. In 1649, the entire population of Kilkenny was cleared out of town by decree. The choice given to the Mayor, Robert Router was the usual one; to hell or to Connacht, but he like the merchants of the town and those of Waterford choose France and settled in Carvin near Arras, in north eastern France.

Returning to Ireland O'Connell joined the Yeomanry Guards, founded to counter the Robert Emmet Rising. He turned away from his Gaelic past; he abandoned the Irish language and derided it. He broke all connections with France and led the Irish into settling for home rule that meant the domination of the country by an English speaking Catholic middle class. The reaction of the Ulster Protestants at the time set the scene for years of problems in the North.

Incidentally, one of the French ambassadors to Britain during the early years of the Revolution was an Irishman named Noel O'Neill.

QUADRAGESIMO ANNO

In the Fortieth Year

Michael O'Brien

Recently, I was just reflecting on the speed with which this year, 1996, was passing and mentally noted some salient features of the months just passed. One important date that flashed through my mind was the day my daughter made her confirmation. I recall the bright happy faces of her and her friends, the joy of parents and grandparents who were happy because the young were happy. This brought me back to my own confirmation day, forty years ago, almost to the month. In the early summer of 1956 I stood trembling before the beady eyes and stern features of the Rev. J.C. McQuaid as he breasted me to ask the Confirmation Question. To my disappointment, he passed me by. I suppose he said to himself "There, but for the grace of God, goes God". On that same day I managed to achieve the second of my burning ambitions - the acquisition of my first pair of long trousers. My first ambition was to acquire a bicycle of my own. This had been fulfilled at Eastertime that same year due to a benevolent uncle. You could say that these were modest ambitions, at least by the standards of today's 12 year olds.

The acquiring of your first long pants suggested that you were starting to face towards young manhood or adulthood. The stock question in the hill country when you were seen in your first 'longers' was "Who lifted you into them?" One was becoming more mature at that time. I started to realise that, for some people, life would always be a bitch and then they would die. I also noticed that the girls in my school were different in a very positive way.

The year 1956 had other similarities with 1996 in so far as the dreary steeples of Fermanagh and Tyrone, that had so haunted Winston Churchill post World War I, were still haunting us in 1956 and continue to do so in 1996. In our mountain school, an irredentist Fior Gael was rehearsing us in the grace notes of the song ' Sean South from Garryown'. In that year I began to realise that the world was not a happy place.

Not all the similarities between '56 and '96 were full of woe. Both years were successful for Ireland at Olympic Games level - with Ronnie Delaney, a man with Arklow connections, claiming gold in 1956 and Michelle Smith winning 3 gold and 1 bronze in 1996. Wexford hurlers were champions in both years also. I suppose it was because Wicklow were not too successful at All-Ireland level that we had to look elsewhere for our sporting Gods. I certainly said my youthful prayers to Nicky Rackard to help fulfil my third burning ambition. As young lads and lassies we arrived home from school more or less at the same time that Cunningham's bread van pulled up at the gate. Not only did he bring the 'loaves and fishes', he also brought the Irish Press. I can still recall gloating over the pages of photographs of the All-Ireland Hurling Final of 1956. I looked on my heroes with the same rapture that my young daughter, today, reserves for Boyzone.

I am not at all conscious of the last weeks of 1956 so I suppose that, for me, there was nothing special about them. The following year, 1957, I fulfilled the last of my trilogy of burning ambitions when I managed to get my first pair of football boots (thanks Nicky). I also passed the Primary Cert. and, just to put the year into the honours category, the Yankee relations came on their one and only Grand European experience and they brought over the famous 'American Parcel'.

MAKE THEM ILLEGAL

John Cassidy

"They make me sick" snorted my perspiring friend who ran into me at the bus station. He paused for a moment to wipe the sweat from his brow, "If the people would only put their foot down they could get them made illegal." This sounded suspiciously like an all-out attack on the Corporation or the Government and I registered agreement by dropping a few nasty cracks about squandering the taxpayer's money and income tax pirates. My guess was wide of the mark however. Neither the government or income tax had put a match to my friend's squib.

The subject of his wrath was the public house clock or, to be more accurate the public house public clock. With childlike faith in one of those benefactors of watchless citizens he had sprinted in alarm for the five thirty express service to Donegal only to find on his arrival at Bus Aras that he had fifteen minutes to spare.

Now the notion of a law against petty annoyance to the citizen will always receive from me a sympathetic ear. It's the petty worries that first plant the crows feet on our youthful complexions and introduce the "grey lock or two in the brown of our hair," and I'm all in favour of rushing a bill through the Dail to suppress them. But there are other things which should be included with the go-as-you-please clocks.

Now we all travel by bus; and considering the vast number of travellers and the general rush and hurry, there are surprisingly few worries connected with this popular means of getting about. But there are one or two items which I would include in my bill. Which of us has not met the man who reads your evening paper over your shoulder? Before the smoking ban was introduced his presence often heralded an unusual warmth on the back of your neck, when lost in your paper he failed to notice that his lighted cigarette was in danger of giving you what your barber often advocates-a hair singe.

However, we must not be too hard on this offender. I must plead guilty to having had an occasional slant at the headlines myself, and he is a mild offender compared to the man on the inside of the only vacant seat, who has peculiar notions as to what share of the seat the person on the outside should claim.

There was a picture in my school book of King John signing the Magna Charta and I always think of that picture when I meet a man on the inside seat. Old John reclined at the table with pen in hand, his left leg sticking out at about the same angle as the sloping edge of a set square, and his general set-up displaying a total indifference to the Barons, who looked as if they would like to sit down.

It is only a few evenings ago I boarded a number ten bus from the City, there was my man on the inside seat, and although the new bus seats could sit two John Hayes in comfort, he had left me for my share about six and a half inches on the outer edge. I sat down with a conciliatory cough which was wasted breath, and retained my bridge head by sticking out my left leg in the gangway as a strut. All went well until an Inspector came along checking tickets and very nearly came a cropper over my stretched leg.

This got my back up against the "inside" and I shifted position with a definite bump; but I might as well have bumped into the Spire in the hope of getting the inside man to change his position.

I had one villainous satisfaction, however; as I bumped in to him I felt rather than heard the ominous crack that indicated that his glasses had gone west. That will teach him I thought to myself with glee. However, I took the precaution of getting off at the stop before the end of my journey, just in case he should put his hand in his pocket for his glasses

Those are only fleeting discomforts of the moment that go with the wind, not so the friend who button-holes you with the query; "What do you fancy for the three-thirty to-morrow."

On confessing that you haven't given it much thought, he gives a quick look around, to see that he is not overheard and then unloads what he describes as "great information" which he has just received from a friend who knows someone in touch with the stables.

It sounds convincing if you are a racing person, and more so if you are not; and while you are wobbling about having a plunge, he pushes you over with the warning (after another look around), "keep it under your hat, and be sure to spread the dough over a few offices so that we won't shorten the price." There is no need to mention the result of this financial transaction. I'd put him in the Bill.

Have you ever got a joyful jolt around about New Years Day, when a postman's double knock on the door requests your signature for a registered letter? Bolting from the breakfast-table or maybe from the bed, you rush to the hall door; perhaps old Uncle Mick has loosened up and has left you his entire estate.

Sliding the lock of the old Yale you stretch out an expectant hand into which is trust a large envelope containing an Income tax demand note. Now tax inspectors are commendably careful in their correspondence, particularly if they are looking for money, but I'd make this stunt illegal under a smart penalty.

These are only a few of the things which would be prohibited by law, if I had my way. No doubt you have a few pet headaches of your own, forward them to me and we will get them in as amendments when my Bill is introduced.

Who cares about the state of the nation or the cost of living, it's the little things which add years to you-as Malarkey said when young Seamus (aged five) and the finest child in the parish, plugged a stone through his kitchen window.

LADY DAY

Declan Gowran

Saint Gabriel announced the mystery
Of a sinless and spotless conception:
A divine statement of love and covenant
Sealed by the knot of the Holy Ghost.

Mary complied with humility, faith and devotion
Much as you did, my love, as I took your body
In my arms, chaste, nude and beautiful like mine
So that together we conceived our first born son
In nervous, tender, blissful innocence and pleasure.

MUCH I KNEW ABOUT NOTHING

Mattie Lennon

A reader asked, Rod Amis, the editor of an On-line maga-
zine, to; "Compliment Mattie Lennon on his ability to
write about nothing". I'm not sure if I have the ability to
write about nothing (which is not the same thing as not having
the ability to write about anything).

When I was made aware of the readers comment I remembered that Pliny the Younger, more than two thousand years
ago, said; "You say you have nothing to write about. Well you
can at least write about that".

Easier said than done. This is my first attempt at it and perhaps I should have taken Francis L. Cornford's advice: "Nothing should ever be done for the first time". Writing at any length
about nothing is not easy. I don't believe I could pen a thousand
words about the contents of my wallet.

I walked myself into this a few weeks ago when I quoted the
late John B. Keane who said that there was no subject under
the sun about which an essay couldn't be written. With all due
respects to the memory of the great Listowel playwright, I don't
recall him ever writing anything about nothing.

So, I may have to let you down. Perhaps after all it's not possible to write about nothing. Although when I was marked in
with the Mucker Graham he claimed that I could fill a Defect-
docket about nothing. Yes, I know many authors and politi-
cian's speechwriters have been accused of writing volumes about
nothing.

Why am I assuming I can do something when so many great
men have failed? According to Samuel Johnson: " George the
First knew nothing, and desired to know nothing: did nothing
and desired to do nothing". Ah, yes, but did he WRITE about
nothing?

As kids in Lacken School we used to define nothing as; "A
bottomless bucket with no sides". But we weren't, as far as I can

remember, ever asked to write an essay about it. Philip Larkin said: "Nothing, like something, happens everywhere". Well, I suppose if it does I'm surrounded by material, if I can find it. When a writer sets out to write about nothing (or in the case of a Dublin writer, "nuttin") the first thing he, or she, needs is a firm knowledge of nothing.

And since a person who knows more and more about less and less is a specialist, what is the term for an expert on nothing?

But then even if I write about nothing will I be writing about nothing. Because Sydney Bernard Smith says; "There is no such thing as nothing after all even if sometimes we seem to be crawling along as a curve at an infinite distance from everything". And Poet/philosopher Pat Ingoldsby pointed out to me that once you start writing about nothing it becomes something. So, maybe that's why scribblers largely neglect nothing; because it doesn't exist. (A bit like the Celtic Tiger).

Yet, when I mentioned it to Eddie McCarthy he gave me great encouragement with: "Yes, one should always write about what one knows".

Mannix Flynn called his autographical work "Nothing To Say" but nowadays even the word nothing doesn't crop up much in titles. In all respects nothing is a neglected subject and those who write about it at all tend to repeat themselves. And those who write about it at all tend to repeat themselves. If the powers-that-be could somehow make nothing a taboo subject only then would it come into its own.

Female hacks in the Sunday Indo would be devoting column yards to it. Vincent Browne would be discussing it and Pat Kenny might even get to hear about it. And yes Eamon Dunphy would be talking about......nothing.

Whew!Charles S. Pierce, the great logician, said in one of his works, in 1898, of nothing; "it is absolutely undefined". He went on the say that the same nothing had; "....unlimited possibility........boundless possibility". I wonder did the bold Charles S. ever sit, at three A.M., after finishing a late duty and try to beat a deadline. Speaking of which, there is a French-polish type product called "Knotting" and I thought I might stick in a few words about it but our Chairman Martin Kenny, said; "No. This has to be about the nothing of negation".

You see with other subjects one can plagiarize, research, redraft and modify. But there is very little source material on nothing. You'd get damn all on it even under the Freedom of Information Act from any Government Department. And that electronic genius, the Net, is great until you type "Nothing" into a search-engine. There's something there about a "Buy Nothing Day" in the US of A and that's about it. And there's no mention at all of it in The World Book.

A Summerhill driver told me in the canteen that John Cage gave a "Lecture on Nothing" in 1961 but I can't find any record of it. "Nothing in Excess" is inscribed on the Temple of Apollo at Delphi. It is variously ascribed to the Seven Wise Men. But (like some of the office Memos that you see) none of them put his name to it. And I hope to God our sponsors don't insist on me putting my name to this.

Staring at a flashing cursor it's hard to agree with Horace that; "To marvel at nothing is just about the one and only thing......that can make a man happy and keep him that way".

I'm sorry. I shouldn't have started this. I should have known that you can't write about nothing. Look at the people who see nothing, hear nothing and apparently experience nothing.... even they can't write about nothing.

So, as William Cowper said;
Defend me, therefore, common sense, say I
From reveries so airy, from the toil
Of dropping buckets into empty wells
And growing old in drawing NOTHING up.

So, I'll stick to what I've been doing; writing FOR nothing.

CHARLIE AND JOHNNY

Declan Gowran

Charlie and Johnny like Laurel and Hardy were the un-likeliest of folk heroes. From the Forties to the Sixties they crewed the Graiguenamanagh to Dublin provincial bus.

Charlie the driver was the jolly fat fellow while Charlie the conductor was somewhat skinny and jumpy. Six days of the week, fair weather or foul, they chugged their route in their two-tone green country bus, usually P-type, through the rich pasturelands of Kildare, Kilkenny and Carlow.

Those were the days of the famous Fighting Cocks of Carlow. Then as now cock-fighting was illegal and it went well with a budding Garda Sleuth to apprehend any of the organisers or competitors. The Fighting Cocks were always transported with the utmost secrecy between the various match venues. All except for Dinny Dangler's fierce cockerel called Red Rascal: he had to be carted First Class by bus in his cat-box. And what's more Dinny would do nothing more than brag about Red Rascal's fighting prowess to any fool who cared to listen.

On Champion's day, Dinny caught the bus to attend the All-Ireland Cock Fight in Carlow. Trailing him in plain clothes, the G-Man followed. True to form Dinny began to extol the fighting qualities of Red Rascal with the G-Man drawing him out and spurring him on. By the time the bus reached Borris, Dinny had spilled the beans.

"I'm arresting you!" The G-Man cried out as he whipped out his I.D. card. "And furthermore, I'm indicting you in the name of Cock-Fighting!"

Charlie heard the commotion in the back of the bus. He deftly swerved, throwing the G-Man off balance. Johnny took his cue from this manoeuvre and shouted: "Run for it!" Dinny made a dash for the door with Red Rascal under his arm and he crying like the crack of dawn. The G-Man followed them and was in a hair's breadth of catching him when Johnny stuck out his foot and tripped him up, sending him sprawling. With that Charlie gunned the engine and sped on, leaving the G-Man in a cloud of exhaust. Dinny escaped. No evidence, no prosecution!

"Couldn't afford to have Dinny incarcerated," Johnny explained later, not when me and Charlie had a quid each on Red Rascal to retain the title!"

They were all dead cute Hoors on the Graiguenamanagh bus. Jimmy Lennon, a local politico from the Borris area, being a prime example. Jimmy used to pay his fare with a note and ask for his change in copper. The 9 AM bus from Graigue would be packed with school kids and as it reached the local national schools, Jimmy would position himself by the door and give each child a coin as they alighted. Any time the kids spotted Jimmy on the bus, there would be a mad stampede for the door to be first off because the kids at the end of the herd couldn't be sure if Jimmy was going to run out of coins before he ran out of eager palms to cross with copper. For some disappointed youngsters, it was a case of better luck next time. This was to teach them not to be doing their exercises on the bus. Their parents would receive positive reports regarding his generosity and he was buying votes for the future.

Back in the old days the country bus was the hub of their universe for many people. It was an era of few cars, fewer trucks and fewer wirelesses. News was moved by word of mouth and if it didn't come by train, it had to come by bus. This news might also be of the harder copy variety and include newspapers, catalogues, magazines and film cans of the latest John Wayne Western from the distributors in Dublin.

The coming and going of the bus was noted with incisive interest by the denizens of the villages and townlands through which it ambled on its progress to and from the Capital. The inquisitive, the crafty farmer, the local gossip all watched diligently, recording the turnover of passengers. They could tell how successful a returning émigré had been by his bearing, by the way he dressed and the angle at his jaw. The Wild Geese they lamented: the poor cut of them with rushed bags and suitcases tied up with string.

Gazing dormantly, these left Ireland with the memory of the final view of home and loved ones etched on their minds through the panorama of a provincial bus window.

These might have been accompanied by chickens and various other miniscule farm animals; for country folk took the bus to market. The saloon was often stacked with boxes of hens, geese and ducklings. While bonhams were the slippiest customers to catch when they escaped from their owner's clutches. At every cross and boreen the intended passengers were found patiently waiting the arrival of the bus. Big Bogmen came down from the mountains with their bicycles in tow. They'd throw them up on the roof with one hand, there to be stowed for the journey to distant relations.

The roof of the bus was Johnny's business. He was the one who had to climb the ladder at the back of the bus and see that all chests, cartons and pushchairs were safely in place. On wet days there was a great tarpaulin supplied to protect the goods from the incessant driving rain and mud of the roads.

When Charlie and Johnny disembarked their passengers at Busarus, they took the bus to Broadstone for a feed of diesel and water and a wash and cleaning. Lunch followed in the canteen or on special occasions like Christmas or birthdays, lunch was taken in the Midland Hotel.

At 5pm on the nose, from Aston Quay, and after 1955 from Bay 13 at Busarus, the bus left for Graiguenamanagh again. How beautiful that name must have sounded to any lost soul going back.

Johnny loved to chat up the passengers. He would often pose them a teaser: "Ye see those pair of ould ewes, sitting yonder," he'd say to some disorientated lad: "If you can tell me their ages, I'll give you back your bus fare as a prize"

All the baffled lad would know was that the women were stout, well girdled in tweeds, sun baked in the face and eating spring onions. "Well if you haven't guessed yet, I'll tell ye: The one sitting on the inside is farty and the other is farty too.... or maybe it's the other way around. Get it? It's the onions ye see!"

First scheduled halt for the bus was Kilcullen. A pit stop in the Hideout where they could see Dan Donnelly's huge skeleton arm in the glass case behind the bar. Dan was the man who beat George Cooper in a bare-knuckles scrap down in Donnelly's Hollow in the Curragh nearby in the year 1815, and he took the unofficial Commonwealth, Empire and World Heavy Weight title as a result of his historic win. Dan was supposed to have the longest reach on record because his arms stretched down to his knees.

So it went on down the line through Moone, Castledermot and Carlow. Borris-in-Ossory was the last scheduled stop before Graigue. The bus always made it in one piece. It was maybe not the swiftest way in the world to do it but it was the safest. When the bus was empty, it was bedded for the night. Johnny swept it, cleaned it and polished it ready for the morning. Charlie checked the engine, that was his department for the oil and the water and he would also check the tyres. All major overhauls were undertaken by Broadstone or Inchicore. Breakdowns, when they occurred, were handled by local depots.

It was traditional for Charlie and Johnny to have a night cap on their way home; "To kill the dust of the road." There was however an obscure rule in the company rule book that prohibited employees from taking intoxicating liquor while in uniform, and sometimes the company sent spies into pubs to catch workers in the act.

In their favourite watering hole, their standing orders were always placed on the bar at the behest of the bar room clock. On this particular night as they arrived in, Johnny approached the bar while Charlie went to the outhouse. For some unknown reason, Johnny froze and held back. He waited for Charlie to come out.

"Don't touch the drink!" Johnny warned Charlie as he reappeared. They left the bar immediately. "How did you cop the company spy" Charlie asked as they were safely outside.

"Twas the bicycle clips!" Johnny explained. "The blessed clips gave him away. No self-respecting, serious drinking countryman would wear his clips to the bar. Not in a church and certainly not in the boozer. He must have been a checker sent over in disguise to catch us. But we copped him!"

Charlie and Johnny were two of nature's gentlemen. They had worth in their community. They provided a vital link with the outside world. Their job was largely routine but they made it entertaining. Theirs was a hum-drum world geared to the changes in the seasons. They cared and took a pride in what they were doing. Perhaps they had more time then and there was less pressure on a body. It was an infinitely slower world then, more evenly paced.

ON GOOD FRIDAY

Paddy Plunkett

All over bar the shouting and that continued outside the doors. It's hard to understand just how much is spent on drink in this country. Everyone has to make their living and this happened to be his, and he was lucky that he had such a thriving business in this day and age. Drink, alcohol kept a lot of people in work in this country for good or ill he mused, from those who make, distribute and sell it to those who have to look after the hurt and pain it causes people.

In the meantime he and his staff wanted to go home to bed and a well earned rest. But not before the takings for the day were counted and the shelves were restocked for the next day's trading which was Saturday. They had ample stock from kegs of beers and stout to bottled beers and a vast amount of spirits. A new record in turnover had been accomplished today, so he was a happy man. Tomorrow was well and truly a day of rest for him and his staff for it was Good Friday.

He then remembered that because they would not be open on Good Friday he had better wind the pub clock, it needed to be wound only once a week and he wound it every Friday. It was old, with roman numerals, and it bore the legend "Ganter Brothers Made in Dublin". He had a great attachment to the timepiece for it was part and parcel of the pub. Just as was the old gas lamp whose mantle was still intact and which was used occasionally if there was a power failure. At the end of the bar was a very large mirror. It too was old and near the top, two opposite semi circles informed you of "De Kuypers Heart Label Gin". It was cracked a little at the bottom from a row that had occurred in the bar many years ago. It too was part of the furniture and fittings of "Dirty Dicks". Satisfied that doors and windows were locked and everything was in order. Paddy the proprietor switched on the alarm bade goodnight to his staff and they went home to their beds for a well earned rest.

Some customers congregated outside gostering and singing, others talking about football and wondering would the Premiership be won over the Easter weekend. All of them knew Good Friday was only a night's sleep away and that it would be the quietest day of the year with the pubs closed all day long. Slowly but surely they went their separate ways all inebriated. "Mind the trams", someone shouted. Christy didn't need to for he went home the short distance to his flat by rail. The individual steel shafts that made up the perimeter railings of the flats he felt carefully until he came to the entrance to the complex he lived in. Once through the gates he found his flat without any bother.

Most of Christy's boozing pals were off to England for Easter. They said they were going over for a match, but if the truth be known they couldn't face Good Friday without the pubs being open. Christy hadn't the money, so he had to stay at home.

Good Friday was a fine bright day and he busied himself doing bits and pieces around the place. He felt a bit seedy and he had a bit of a hangover but he felt a bit better as the day wore on. A long day seemed to turn into an even longer evening His missus was going over to Whitefriar Street to do the Stations of the Cross. He thought he might go with her and pass a bit of time. He thought again. No, too long and drawn out.

He thought back to past Good Fridays. They always seemed to be cold, wet and miserable with nothing to do. The only place to go was to play football up in the fifteen acres and in the evening go over to the Mansion House to see the European Cup Final on film. It was the same match shown year after year. He remembered the seats in the round room torn, and with the horsehair sticking out of them. But it was the match. That was the magic bit. Good Friday in the Mansion House was Hamden Park 1960. 135,000 people Real Madrid versus Eintracht Frankfurt. Oh he loved saying the name Eintracht. It sounded really different, really foreign. The screen was tiny sixteen millimetre film. But there was a full house. Every year there seemed to be more scratches on the print than the year before. And the click, click, click of the projector seemed noisier. What a match final score Real Madrid;7, Eintracht Frankfurt;3. Magical goals from fabulous players 4 for Puskas 3 for Di

Stefano of Real Madrid and players named Kress and Stein scored for Eintracht.

Despite his fond memories he was becoming slightly agitated. He missed the pub. It was too early to touch his few cans he had put away, never the less he checked them and made sure they were still intact. He put on his jacket and the lead on his beloved dog Brandy. It was obvious to anyone who saw Brandy that he was a mongrel. Christy would have none of it. As far as he was concerned he was a pure "ton a bred" but what he really meant was ' thoroughbred'. They walked towards Stephens Green, crossed at the Unitarian Church and made their way along the tree lined west side of the park where the Luas operates from. As they approached the midway point, where the statue to Lord Ardilaun is, Brandy let out a yelping cry. The dog was petrified. He picked him up. There didn't seem to be anything physically wrong with him, and there was no other animal or person about. He set him down on the ground again and as he got up he looked in at the monument. Lord Ardilaun, Arthur Edward Guinness was no longer there. Christy closed his eyes tightly, and opened them again and looked. The monument was complete in every detail. The plinth, the chair he sat on, even the grass surrounding it was freshly mown. He was definitely not there. Christy felt an eerie feeling within himself. They quickly made their way down York Street, which is opposite the monument. He'd surely meet someone he knew here. Not a sinner. Like the dog Christy felt insecure. The city had a ghost like feel to it.

"Drink, I need a drink," he said to himself. He made his way home as quickly as he could but not before he passed Dirty Dicks. There was an old handcart outside over the cellar gates. He hadn't seen one of those in years, yet it was familiar. He thought he saw a glimmer of light through the blinds. He went to the bar door, looked around. His heart pounding he put a slight pressure on the door. To his surprise it opened and he entered. The gas mantle behind the bar was glowing brightly. The pub was packed yet different. There were drinks everywhere and a great atmosphere pervaded the place. The clientele were not locals yet Christy seemed to know almost all of them.

He saw a man at the bar that seemed down on his luck. From the back he vaguely recognised him. He had bird droppings on his hair and shoulders. His long dirty coat and boots had a greenish bronze hue about them. He made his way over to him, he touched his coat it had a cold metallic feel to it. A button fell from the back belt of his coat. Christy picked it up and put it in his pocket. The man lifted a pint of Guinness from the counter and drank it down. The metallic look and bird droppings disappeared. What emerged was a friendly moustached face with bright sparkling eyes and a cheerful smile. Transformed he was dressed impeccably. He introduced himself. Christy could hardly contain himself, for this was the man who was missing from his chair in Stephens Green. Lord Ardilaun, Arthur Edward Guinness. Christy offered him a stool, he refused it, saying he didn't mean to be rude but he had a pain in his arse sitting on the same seat in the Green for over a hundred years. So if he didn't mind he'd prefer to stand and have a drink and a chat with him. He told Christy that he loved Dublin and that it was great to be back in body even if it was only for a short period of time. He also explained to him that what he was encountering was the Dublin Monumental Statue Movement Meeting. And that these meetings were held only once in a blue moon.

A monumental reunion it might have been for Lord Ardilaun but those he introduced to Christy seemed to be there in body, mind and spirit. They were a Who's Who of Dublin monuments. They were all there; Poets, Literary Geniuses, Politicians, Trade Unionists, Rebels, Chancers, Musicians. The Famine Hungry. The Tart with the big heaving bosom who had left her handcart outside was there too, attracting a lot of attention from the former great and good. Surgeon Park who normally resides outside the "Dead Zoo" on Merrion Square was chatting to a Frankenstein monster like Wolfe Tone. Father Matthew was going around imploring them all to give up the demon drink, but was not having much luck. James Joyce was singing "The Lass of Aughrim". Phil Lynott said "Christy remember the craic we used to have in the 5 Club in Harcourt Street."He sure did. The Two ladies who sit with their Arnotts's bags beside the Halfpenny Bridge were still chatting, but here in the pub, and having a drink. They all said that they missed Lord Nelson on his pillar. His head which was on the end of the bar smiled wryly. Keeping them all under control was the Chief Usher, whose residence is outside the Screen Cinema in Hawkins Street. He was complete with his trusty torch and was dressed in all his fine regalia. Drinking and merriment was the order of the day. Christy could take no more of this surreal world he had entered. He bid Lord Ardilaun and all his monumental friends goodnight. He went home with Brandy who now was in great form wagging his tail, and went straight to bed.

Were they coming to take him away was his first thought as his wife woke him from a very deep sleep. The reflection of blue flashing lights covered the ceiling of the bedroom. He shivered a little and heard the din of what sounded like fire engine pumps. He dressed in a flash and ran down to the street. Dirty Dicks was no more. A huge fire had engulfed the building and reduced it to rubble. Ace reporter Charlie Swan the nations favourite hack, back from a sojourn in the United States was in vintage form. He described the fire as been Ghoulish, Unbelievable, Bizarre and Unprecedented. That it was. The Gardai and fire crews, who fought the inferno, ruled out arson as a cause, as fire brigade personnel had to break down the doors and windows to get to fight the blaze. Their investigations revealed that not a drop of drink was left in the pub. All the kegs, bottled beers and spirits were mysteriously now empty. Despite the massive temperatures and the millions of gallons of water used to extinguish the fire, they found intact and in perfect working order the pub clock, the De Kuypers Mirror and the old gas lamp.

Christy went onto the small veranda of his flat. He fed the birds a few crumbs and crusts of bread. He sneezed, took his handkerchief from his pocket and as he did so he pulled something with it which fell to the ground. He bent down and picked it up. What had been an old dirty button was now a bright gold one with A. E. Guinness inscribed on it.

WHO WERE THE BLACK AND TANS?

Scotty Sturgeon

Said Lloyd George to McPherson I'll give you the sack,
To uphold law and order you have not the knack,
I'll send over Greenwood he is a much better man
And I'll fill the Green Isle with the bold Black and Tans.

Apart from the word famine, or the name Oliver Cromwell, few terms aroused such horror, and hatred amongst the Irish as did the Black and Tans. When the I.R.A. campaign against the R.I.C. [Royal Irish Constabulary] became more violent and successful in late 1919, the police abandoned hundreds of rural facilities and retreated to fortified stations.

The pressure exerted on the R.I.C. men, their families, friends and those who did business with them resulted in unfilled vacancies from casualties, resignations and retirements. Faced with the need for more, better-prepared men, the British Government began recruiting Great War veterans from throughout the U.K.

From March 1920 through to the truce in July 1921, 13,732 new police were added to the Old R.I.C. to maintain a police strength that, at the end reached 14,500. The I.R.A. campaign led to another recruitment initiative in July 1920, the Auxiliary Division, former military Officers who wore Tam O'Shanter caps and acted in counter-insurgency units independent of other police units.

Even though the Auxiliaries were a separate unit were generally known as Black and Tans.

This notorious corps who wore kaki tunics and black trousers were called after a famous Irish hunting pack, they lived up to this title ravaging the countryside and firing at will at anything that moved in field or street. The philosophy behind this counter-insurgency force was that reprisals for I.R.A. actions would make the community willing to yield up the guerrillas; it had the opposite effect, the people turned towards, not against, the guerrillas for protection and counter-reprisal.

So who were these people and where did they come from? The Commander of the Black and Tans was Major General Sir Hugh Tudor. Sir Hugh's other claim to fame in military history is as inventor of the smokescreen during the trench warfare of the first World War, when he was Commander of the Ninth Scottish Division. It was said of him he was given a dirty job to do in Ireland and he pushed dirty war tactics to the limit. When General Crozier suspended twenty six members of the Black and Tans sister force, the Auxiliary Cadets, for their part in burning the town of Trim in February 1921, Tudor reinstated them.

The Black and Tans and Auxiliaries were overwhelmingly British almost two thirds were English, fourteen were Scottish and fewer than five percent came from Wales. Amazingly more than 2,300 Black and Tans and 225 of all Auxiliaries were Irish. Sixty percent of them came from the provinces of Ulster and Leinster and forty percent from the provinces of Munster and Connacht.

Eighty percent of 'Tans' were Protestant, seventeen percent were Catholic, and there were ten English Jews. The most dangerous County for them to serve in was Cork where at least 119 of them were wounded and 90 killed.

When the R.I.C. was disbanded in 1922 all those still serving were given life time pension.

The annual payment for each man varied between fifty-five pounds for those who served the longest and forty-seven pounds for the most recent recruits.

What of Commander Hugh Tudor? After being relieved of his Irish command Tudor picked Newfoundland as being a place where the long arm of the I.R.A. would not reach. He lived quietly by himself working in the fish business unmolested by anyone, although it is recorded in his obituary that; there were times when proceeding to supervise the loading of fish; he was compelled to run a gauntlet of biting commentary from Irish crewmen.

Despite his low profile his presence in Newfoundland became known to the I.R.A, and two men were sent to assassinate him. Being good Catholics they went to confession first. When one of them asked for absolution for the killing he was about to carry out, the priest sought a few details. Having weighed up the situation the priest gave the gunman two pieces of information.

First was the good news, he would give him absolution and there was no doubt he and his companion would be able to carry out their mission successfully. Then came the bad news. The priest asked whether the would-be assassins had given much thought to their getaway?

They had realised of course that Newfoundland was an Island? The would-be killers admitted the answer to both questions was no. The priest pointed out that the killing of Sir Hugh would be followed by two further executions, their own. They had assumed that Newfoundland was part of the Canadian mainland.

Sir Hugh lived to a ripe old age. He died, blind and alone, at St John's Hospital on the 26th September 1963, at the age of ninety-five. His wife, two daughters and son never joined him from England. He was laid to rest in Forest Road Anglican cemetery, St John's. His grave is marked by a two-foot pink/marble stone, inscribed only with his name, rank dates of birth and death.

THE ARTIST

Anthony Doyle

I look into the room of light and dark,
Colours paint a rainbow
Along the walls of beauty,
How they hold many novels
Waiting to be read
By those who dare to travel
Into the canvas of another's expression.

The deeper you go
The more you reach the contours
These fences of a fastidious exuberant heart
A mind and soul racing
In the strokes of brush
The waiting times of pause held
Waiting for some message from the gods

To call forth the image
That is waiting on the edge of the mind
Upon the wings of the unicorn
To wave its feathers of brown in the colour
That makes the red the colour of blood
Its fire is felt and seen
In the boldness of its own defining presence

A measure of sacrifice
A measure of a feminine month
In the birth canal of vision as life is delivered
To empty the womb, to hold the empathy of life.
Papers waiting on the dresser,
Scattered on the folding mat
Whose cornered tongue shows signs of speech?

To tell the looker to look deeper
Into the pencil marks
These glances in the black and white
But laced and layered upon an infinite land
Where imagination and divine light has shone
A witness to his craft
To dance inside and out

Of this world that holds creativity as sacred
Open to all who open their hearts and minds
For those who dare to invite the force of life
The force of death into their lives
That brings the precise the edge
All the more nearer,
Where life reaches its fragile nature of the mortal

The immortality that is the promise
In the canvas beyond the impression of skin
Into the vessel of the heavens
The winged ships of the gods
Who fly in the face of conventionality
Who smile at deaths relevance
In arched chair

He sits in a long soft poise
Relaxed in the infirmity of the creative space
Balancing his grounded ness with the vision of expansion
A mind and heart's strings stretching
Such taught ness and insider fighting is not witnessed
It is known
By the hand of another

Who plots and marks the same nautical path
Upon the maritime maps of an normal abnormality
Not contented by convention
That is for some souls imprisoned in their skin of earth;
Bounded by a life led by a lead a chain of limiting
To stop the ship
That is their soul

From ever leaving the harbour
And moving out into the ocean of existence
This place where life has its being
Where the substance and value of one's life are routed.
His hair is flounced
Waves colliding in a coil like expression
Natures black thorn and bramble touching

Making a hedge row on a human mantle of thought.
A grey wind cuts through his sides
Searching I feel for the top
To show to one and all the winter of his years,
Age has found softness in his face
Gentle folds as furrows of a field
Exposed to the plough of thought

Are harrowed back by a gentle hand
Guiding his life through the night and day
Blending hardship and harmony together as one.
Hands have found their infancy again
Clay from the morning's soft toil with Adam
Have left some measure upon his palms and fingers
One and the same.

The cotton pinstripe sticks out its cuff
From underneath the suit of a once distant newness,
Now aged
But never did it loose its style
Its taste is that of the timeless
A clothing succulence devoid of fashions fiasco
An elegance in the manufactured care

Made to last
Not a superficial rag
From a trade lost to consistency of quality.
Where starved women parade to the world
The brand and make up of the starving rich
Holding to the young women
A picture devoid of beauty or depth but one hunger.

Sounds move me
A tick so gentle, yet present
Is heralded from the place of silences vibrancy
A soft tone that moves
With the rhythm of the room
Carrying its emotion

In the cradle of a petal
Holding its seed of thought close
As only a maternal mother could.
Such an objective and one of unconditionality
A space where the mind is free
To listen to the words echoed from the heart

Where spirit speaks to man
As never before.
Where the idleness of chatter is abated
And truth and wisdom flow
As a winter's river racing
To meet her lover in the sea of dreams.
I look a little further down

A chic press
Holding its own with time
Makes a giant of an impression
To this room of a historical making
Where substance is gathered from nothingness
A philosopher's stone of alchemy
Placing art as the corner stone of creativity.

DIP ME FLUTE

Mattie Lennon

Long before DeValera expressed his dream of "comely maidens and athletic youths at crossroads" young people held crossroads dances at Kylebeg in the West Wicklow of my youth. At the time it was the equivalent of Facebook or Plenty-of-Fish.

There was the occasional "American Wake" 'though not described as such in our part of the country. And during the twenties and thirties there were also a number of regular dancing houses; usually dwellings with flagged floors and one or more eligible daughters. The small two-roomed home of John Osborne was one such house. Situated at the hill ditch, which divided the common grazing area of "The Rock" from the relatively arable land. There was no road to the house.

It was accessible only through the aptly named "Rock Park"; the nocturnal negotiation of this field was a feat even for the most sure-footed. This had one advantage; when the Free State government introduced the House Dance Act of 1935 which banned dances, dancers and musicians. You had to get a license to hold a dance even in your own house. They came up with a moral argument against dancing and ....if you don't mind . . a sanitary facilities argument. But as one commentator said, at the time, "the Government don't care if you make your water down the chimney as long as they get their money." But a breach of the law could result in a court appearance and penalty.

However there was no danger of a late night invasion of John Osborne's by any Government Inspector. Because even the most dedicated servant of the State would not risk a nightime ambulation through the Rock Park. As the shadows jumped on the whitewashed walls and the lamplight flickered on the willow patterned delph an official invasion was the furthest thing from the minds of the revellers.

John Osborne, the man of the house was an accomplished flautist. Did he, I wonder, favour saturating his instrument, like, Neddy Bryan, the flute-player from Ballyknockan, who on arrival at a session would request the facility to "....dip me flute in a bucket o' water?.".

According to the older people, Neddy Bryan,. . . when he was a young man played the Piccolo . . .that is . . . until the local schoolmaster informed him that the name Piccolo came from Piccolo Fluato . . the Italian for a "small flute". "I'm damned" says Neddy "If I'm going to be called the fella with one of thim things" and from then on he concentrated on the *larger* flute. Neddy was a fair enough flute player but John Osborne would get so engrossed by certain tunes that he would go into a sort of a trance.

One night he was after playing a tune called "High Level" (Now . . .if I was sworn I can't remember if it was a jig or a reel). Anyhow, one of the boyos says to him, "Do you know that your daughter is abroad in the haggard with Jimmy Doyle?" "I don't" says John "But if you whistle a few bars of it I'll have a go at it".

Dancing wasn't the only thing that went on in such houses. If John Osborne was alive today he would be described as eccentric. Well . . . I suppose he wouldn't . . he was a poor man and you have to be well off to merit the euphemism "eccentric". Anyway, he was a bit odd but could have some very practical, if unorthodox solutions to certain situations. I'll give you an example. One night a visiting dancer; a fine young fellow who had the "book-learnin" was going the next day for an interview with a view to joining the Garda Siochana. Opinions were divided as to whether he was of the required height. Until a horse dealer, a relation of my own, stated with some authority,

"That man is not the full eighteen hands high".

Paddy Toomey a stone cutter who only lived one field away went home and returned with a six-foot rule. And sure enough the prospective Guardian-of-the-peace proved to be half an inch short of the required height. What was to be done?. This was before the era of "brown envelopes" and anyway times were poor. John Osborne hit on a plan. When the dancer's back was turned he dropped his flute and with the maximum alacrity picked up an ash-plant. Almost before the pause in the music was noticed he gave the young man a belt of the stick on top of the head. "A fellandy" it was called up our way. The man in question had a good thick head o' hair and the resulting bump brought him up to the required height.

He made a good Guard but ever after, in our area anyway, he was known as "lumpy head". There were some colourful nicknames around our place, One young male patron of Osborne's was known as "you'll have yer ups an' downs". You are going to ask me how anyone could end up with such a cumbersome handle. Well . . . I'll tell you. It was inherited- like a Peerage. His father, as a young man had met a girl at a house-dance, a few miles away. Her parents were dead and she had returned from the US of A and, of course, had a few Dollars. And she was an only child, into the bargain and had inherited a good few acres. Me man played his cards well and told her a few stories that wouldn't exactly run parallel with the truth. Anyway, to make a long story short, the relationship blossomed and they got married. He was a steady enough lad . . . he had a few head o' cattle . . . five or six. But . . . he had five brothers and each of them had a good few cattle. . . which he borrowed for the occasion. (In modern Banking parlance such a move would be described as," an artificial boost".) The new bride must have thought she was back in the land of extensive ranches when the herd was installed on her little farm. There were Shorthorns, Friesians, Whiteheads and a couple of Aberdeen Anguses. Needless to say, for the first few mornings after the wedding the young couple didn't get up too early. But one morning when the new bride arose from the marriage bed she noticed a reduction in the herd. One of her brothers-in-law, under cover of darkness, had repossessed what was rightfully his. When she pointed out the loss to her spouse his only comment was "you'll have your ups an' downs". "You'll have yer ups an' downs"

Every other night a similar raid would take place as each brother took back his livestock and every time the moryah "innocent" husband would say "you'll have yer ups an' downs"

But I'm rambling. nowadays I think they call it digressing. I mentioned earlier about the practice of dipping the wooden flute in water. Well, whether for flute-immersion or not a galvanized bucket of water was a permanent feature on the stone bench outside Osborne's door. And one June night when the boys and girls (a term used to describe those unmarried, and under 70) having made it, relatively unscathed through the Rock Park, were knocking sparks from the floor. They were glad of the opportunity, amid the jigs and the reels (and God only knows what other energy-sapping activities) to exit occasionally for a refreshing draught from the Parnassian bucket.

At day-break, while preparing to depart, the exhausted assembly was informed by a youth (who was looked on locally as "a sort of a cod") of how he had suffered during the night with a stone-bruise on his big toe. The pain, he said, would have been unbearable but for the fact that; " I used to go out now an' agin an' dip it in the bucket o' water".

A DONEGAL CHRISTMAS

Liam McCauley

Every Christmas is a special time for many different reasons. In recent years, I have had the benefit of learning from those who lived in other countries how the story of Christmas can differ slightly, what way the festivities are celebrated can vary and how even the dates of importance can be substantially different. Nevertheless the one thing which all have in common is the family and children, around which it all revolves.

For many of us in Ireland an ideal Christmas is a white one, not a common event in Ireland with our mild climate which seldom stretches to snow, especially when you might be tempted to wish for it. So although snow was unlikely, as children growing up in south Donegal in the 1960's we knew hope was important and it became part of our other expectations and preparations in the lead up to the big day.

One of the differences we had was that in a time where the pace of life was a little slower, Santy's journey could be carried out in the blink of an eye, but such was the number of houses he had to visit that he still did not manage to get to part of south Donegal until nearly the end of morning Mass on Christmas Day. So no matter how much we would like to we were not likely to ever be in place to actually see this fascinating character.

Preparations were all important, letters were written and re-written, as other tasks were completed to ensure the qualifying good behaviour was obvious and unquestionable.

Getting the chimney cleaned was a crucial job otherwise he would get his famous red suit soiled and blackened on the turf soot. A chimney brush was fashioned from a blackthorn bush and with a rope tied to either end, one man standing on top of the thatched roof, the other beside the fireplace, as the "brush" was pulled up and down, each, doing their best to create as little mess as possible.

All this in the hope that the boys would get the cowboy gear they wanted, the girls all the dolls and the all important compendium of games which would last through every rainy Sunday for the rest the year and all this would be waiting for us when we got home.

One particularly special Christmas morning when I was about 6 or 7 is particularly memorable, for as soon as we awoke, we realised from the brightness outside that it had snowed overnight. There was perfect snow everywhere, at least 5 or 6 inches of it, on the fields, every hedge, every branch of every tree had its own picture postcard share to display. Were we allowed out to play in it? Not a bit, it was Christmas morning and we were quickly reminded about putting on our best clothes and boots or shoes for Mass which would start only too quickly. There would be plenty of time for play later.

Besides, the house also had to be vacated for our important visitor as well. Our chapel was a quick half mile walk away and in no time at all, other families making the same journey were filtering along the road towards our house. Before long, about 9 or 10 children were speculating about what kind of car, truck, cowboy gear, doll or pram might await us later, eyes wide with the thought of eventually getting to play in the virgin crunchy snow.

We began making our way, excitement barely under control, above us our breath steamed in the crisp air, behind us the occasional adult hurrying to catch up after doing last minute things, around us, the other adults doing their best to ensure we did not get too carried away, throwing snowballs and so on. Suddenly, the entire world stopped, there along the road in front of us, carved into the clean canvas of snow, were an undisputable set of tracks of a small twin hoofed animal.

Now, we had never seen a reindeer other than in storybooks but we all knew that on that particular morning there was only one animal that could possibly, have made those tracks. Without saying a word, every child in that group looked at each other, reading each other's minds, as we all realised the same thing, there right in front of us for the entire world to see were the footprints of Santy's reindeer, a wonder that children everywhere longed to see but the story was, never got to see, no more than the great man himself.

Whatever control we had been under up to that point, disappeared in a flash, as all began jumping, shouting and roaring about our wonderful, joyous and unexpected find. In the middle of trying to restore some order, one practical farmer, forgetting that he was once a child himself, pointed out that it was probably just a sheep or calf that had gotten out from where it should be. However as we quickly glanced around the familiar fields with names like Crockasturry and Lugnaminna, of all mornings there was not a single animal of any description to be seen.

In the split second it took for us to check all this, then once again, looking at each other, we could see in each other's faces that it didn't matter if the grown up's believed us or not because WE KNEW. Yes we knew what those tracks were with that unshakeable faith and hope of children.

That was a very special Christmas for many different reasons; I now understand that with more modern technology Santy can now reach south Donegal much earlier, even during the early hours of Christmas day.

Whether we have lost or gained something in that is for others to decide, but many of the people whose faces are still so fresh in my memory of that day, have themselves passed on, leaving those of us who are still growing up, to help create new Christmas memories through stories or deeds, for those in the earlier stages of growing up. To misquote the words of another "Memories and differences can come and go but Christmas remains the same".

ALIEN INTERVENTION

Thomas Carroll

The year is 2090. It's now ten years since the friendly aliens known as Zendonians arrived on planet earth. In that period of time humans have acquired a vast amount of knowledge from these beings. Thanks to the Zendonian's space-age technology we now have computer chips which grow inside our brains enabling us to reason at a phenomenal speed. The average human can now calculate complex mathematical equations in a matter of seconds. Our intelligence has become superhuman.

Alien technology means we no longer eat food three times a day. A vito-nutro tablet provides all our daily requirements. There is one disadvantage – we must drink a minimum of ten gallons of water per day. This is necessary to flush out our supercharged bodies and brains.

The Zendonians willingly offered a longer life span of one hundred years to anyone who wanted this opportunity. About twenty per cent of humans accepted. This offer was conditional – humans receiving this gift would have to travel to the alien planet of Zenda which was twelve billion light years away in the galaxy of Genesis X. Here they would live out the extra one hundred years of their lives.

Back on earth the Zendonians have eliminated poverty, food shortage and mankind's obsession with war. All this has meant the prospect of an improved future is now a reality for third world countries. Next the Zendonians are going to tackle crime, violence and greed. If these three unbalances are successfully removed, our society will be almost perfect. Imagine being able to walk the streets without the fear of violence. The wealthy classes assisting the less well-off to maintain a decent standard of living; which will in turn remove the cycle of poverty and crime.

Alien intervention has enabled mankind to create a fantastic new world; thus ensuring that our descendents will inherit a society of joy and goodness.

THE HANGOVER

Mattie Lennon

Here's a story told to me by a cousin, in Ballinastockan, who wouldn't know how to tell a lie. It's about a local man who was nicknamed "the Mouse" and here are the cousin's exact words,

"The Mouse was a great man to knock down drink. But to my mind the time that his alcoholic acumen came into its own was on one Tuesday morning . . it was after a Bank holiday weekend and he was badly in need of a hair of the dog. (As far as I cam remember that was the morning he said to his own dog, "bite me if you like but don't bark") On the morning in question his total finances amounted to one solitary English truppeny bit. Do you remember them? Anyway the English truppeny bit was brass and twelve sided. There's a word for that. An oul schoolmaster told me once. It's Dod . . dod . . . me oul head is goin.Dodecagonal. Dodecagonal . Where was I? Oh yes. The mouse an' the truepenny bit. Now, even though things were cheap at the time it would take five shillings, or a half a crown at the very least to make any impression on a hangover. So what could a man do with a truepenny bit? I couldn't do anything with it. An' I bet you couldn't do much with it either. But the mouse had a plan. The price of a clay pipe, at the time, was truppence. So . . he went to Burke's shop, in Lacken, an' he purchased a new clay pipe.

Head splittin' . . . mouth like the inside of a septic tank and the nerves in bits . . and now . you are going to ask me what good a clay pipe . . even a new one . .would be to alleviate such a condition. Well . . .at the time it was believed that a clay pipe had to be seasoned. The favoured method was to fill the pipe-bowl with whiskey . . . something that even the most parsimonious publican couldn't very well refuse to supply.

Armed with his new pipe, the mouse headed for Blessington and into Hennessy's where he asked the barman to fill his

111

purchase with the necessary amber liquid which he promptly sucked out through the stem. He visited Miley's, Powers and Dowlings with the same request. And then he crossed the street to Mullally's and the Gunch Byrnes. He got a bonus in the Gunche's . . he managed to get a fill in the bar and the lounge. You with the mathematical turn of mind will know that the bowl of a clay pipe would hold approximately 8 ml and if you were paying attention you'd know that he got it filled seven times which would amount to a sum total of 56 millilitres of whiskey. I won't bore you with the exact conversion to imperial measure; you went to school as long as I did but . . the total alcohol involved amounted to slightly more than a small one. Hardly enough to make inroads into a severe, seasonal, hangover. But it was a start. . and . . as luck would have it the Mouse got a lift to Naas where . . at the time there were thirty seven pubs."

TIN WHISTLE

Ronnie Hickey

I will not play my whistle;
It's nice that you should ask
You say it gives you pleasure,
To me it is a task.

In the confines of my little shed,
With door and window locked,
I sit and toot on my tin flute
And frequently am shocked;
After all the hours of practice,
My musical brain half dead,
Fingers fluttering in half terror
Anticipating their next error;
This awful lack of confidence
I'd rather not display.

But sometimes, playing all alone
The notes come pouring out;
They thrill the room
Dispatch the gloom
And lift me to a mystical height,
So wild the tune I want to shout
I've made it I can do it

So maybe I should play for you,
Share my sometimes gift,
When it works we'll dance for joy
Pretend we're hearing Matt Molloy.
Or James Galway's golden tone
May lift us to a higher zone.
With nerve endings all abristle
Hand me down that new tin whistle
And, fingers trembling with aggression
Commence a fabulous new session.

AN ONLY CHILD

Mattie Lennon

I haven't ever been described as the black sheep of the family.....and that's simply because I am an only child. Do my traits, foibles and way of living reflect the fact that I was reared as an only child? In the late nineteenth century Alfred Adler, the founder of Individual Psychology, indicated the importance of a child's position in the "family constellation". According to present day experts here are some common personality traits of "only children":

Confident: Only children are usually not afraid to make decisions and are comfortable with their opinions.

Pays Attention to Detail: They like things to be organized and are often on time.

Good in School: Onlies tend to read a lot and have a good memory for facts and figures.

IT'S MINE!: Only children might have difficulty sharing or going second because they have always been first in line for everything.

Overly Critical: While being a perfectionist is not such a bad thing, you may have a tendency to take this to extremes and be really critical of yourself and others. If you're an "only," these feelings may be familiar:

"I didn't do as well as I should have." "Sometimes I feel lonely." "I would be much happier with a brother or sister." "I'm not getting enough attention." Even though, as an only child, you probably spend a lot of time talking with your parents; do you make sure you express yourself to them about any long-term feelings that get you down?

Professor Floy Pepper of Portland, Oregon, said " The only child has a decidedly difficult start in life as he spends his entire childhood among persons who are more proficient. He may try to develop skills and areas that will gain approval of the adult world or he may solicit their sympathy by being shy, timed or helpless".

The Professor goes on to say that the only child is usually pampered -and if a boy has a mother complex who feels that his father is his rival.

He enjoys his position as a centre of interest and is, usually, interested only in himself. He sometimes has a feeling of insecurity due to the anxiety of his parents. Since the only child, for the most part, is not taught to gain things by his own effort, merely to want something is to have it. If his requests are not granted, he may feel unfairly treated and refuse to cooperate.

Some time ago I came up with the mad notion of forming an International Association of Singletons. My idea fell flat on its face. Only three or four only children showed any interest. Most of them seem to want to get on with their lives. I did however get a lot of views from "onlies" worldwide who had varied views (most of them positive) on their birth order.

Hai Rud in France said:"...I feel almost privileged to be without any brothers and sisters...when I was eight or nine years old I remember an elderly neighbour patting me on the head and telling me not to worry-my mother would provide me with some company soon! My reaction was one of complete indifference to the possibility: I felt neither relieved nor jealous at the prospect, there was a complete blank in my mind".

And the effect in later life?. "I dislike large groups of people, even friends, when you have to talk loudly to be heard. As an only child, when you say something your parents listen to you and devote their attention to you. There is not therefore the competition to be heard or taken notice of. I see the result of this today in that I will not "fight" to the front of a conversation...My partner is also an only child. What is interesting is that neither of us will have a full scale fight over anything- we both tend to retreat rather than battle it out, simply because we never had to fight with a brother or sister..."

Karen Jiudetti, from Massachusetts, claimed that; "...being an only child helped me become very independent...has created in me a certain capacity of meditation, as well as a greater sense of reason, call it pragmatism. I feel I matured mentally earlier than others of my age".

Laurie S. Potter, Santa Barbra, California felt "...the positive aspects of being the only child were many. She says her parents; "...generally tried to give a life they never had." She mentions a couple of drawbacks, ("it gives a child a very narrow frame of reference. The frame is rigid with so few people in the picture") but sums it up as follows; "all in all it was a good experience and fostered a feeling of independence."

Not all singletons are as thankful for their birth order. Mrs Shirley Parker-Munn from Wales (whose mother and grandmother were both only children) told me; "Being an only child was terrible. Much loneliness, no allies and totally in a dominant, adult orientated world I couldn't relate properly to other children...I hated my childhood...I still feel like a freak because everyone around one has siblings and I do not."

Eileen Bowman, London, felt responsible for the welfare of her parents as they got older and she says: "I did not have the confidence to be able to deal with people. I always felt on the periphery and not able to make friends too easily". She feels that being an only child; "...makes one a loner which is not always of one's choosing".

Fotios Papazopulos, a Greek, told me: "My childhood life was lonely and rarely oppressive...it created me some problems later in life. I was shy with women, introvert and not socialising with others until I got to know them well at which point I liked to monopolise the attention...I paired up with a woman whom I met through the mail. It proved disastrous under any aspect".

Of all the only children who contacted me Mr. Papazopulos was, as far as I can recall, the only one who had a completely negative approach to his birth order. How do only children fare in the marriage stakes? It is claimed that the marriage of two only children is the least likely to last.

Well, I married an only child and she has tolerated me for three decades. I mean it has to have advantages . . . think of the absence of in-laws!

LIKE FRED AND GINGER

Ronnie Hickey

We glide
Slow,
Quick, quick slow,
On longing strides
And turn and close
In expectation
Of something new.
Spaces loom
And disappear
In bodies blur
As perfume whirls.
We plunge and swerve
To another time
Of shoulder, hip
And touching shoe
On a shimmering
Never ending cloud
Of elemental joy.

THE REVENGE OF THE LOTTO
WINNING GOLFER

Christy Butler

It was a bleak miserable night in November, in the final year of the Millennium, as I approached the public phone box. A storm had arrived on our shores and it seemed an appropriate time to commence 'Operation Revenge'. I had spent many hours in its planning and felt confident that I could pull it off in style. It was close to midnight.

On entering the phone box. Close to my home, I lifted the receiver and dialled the number of the local undertaker. Mobile phones are traceable. Safety lies in the public call box.

Brrr, brrr. Answer before I lose my nerve I thought.

"Good night, Michael Donovan speaking, how can I help you?"

"Good night to you Mr Donovan" I said, in a quivering solemn voice. "There's been a death in the family".

I sighed.

"My brother, Onty, has died. Could you call at 9 AM in the morning, with your hearse and remove the remains to your funeral home in Sallynoggin and make the necessary arrangements", I said.

I continued.

"It was expected and I have a Doctors certificate".

"Very good Sir" he replied and requested the address.

"79 Leopardstown Creek", I answered in my best Dublin 4 accent. A touch of class was needed and I also needed to be convincing.

"May I have your name Sir?" he requested

"Strichy Reltub" I said. "I also need a wreath with the message coded".

I supplied the details.

"Thank you for calling us Mr Reltub. I shall take care of everything and be with you in the morning at 9 AM. Good night now and take care", said Mr Donovan.

"You too", I said and replaced the phone on its cradle. All was set. I returned home and treated myself to 3 fingers of Middleton Reserve whiskey. That will fix Bastárd, I thought, and Onty. (Bastárd, alla Franca, with an á is my other brother's nickname). My brothers Onty and the Bastárd live together in Leopardstown Creek. Hopefully they will be 'up the creek' at 9 tomorrow morning, if my plan is fulfilled.

But there you are sitting on a Bus, LUAS or DART. You maybe on your way home or even going to work. You have started to read this story and suddenly you are wondering what the hell is going on! You have a perfect right to think this and toss the book into the nearest bin.

For I can see that I have started against common sense, at the end. Now I am not much of a storyteller and common sense tells me to commence at the beginning. So here goes. Enjoy.

But first, my dear reader, I must warn you that names have been changed to protect the idiots and the innocent, mentioned in this story. I have endeavoured to construct anagrams of the names, for the more cultured among you. For the cryptologists among you, have some fun as well.

Here we go.

My name is STRICHY RELTUB. Every year, in mid-September, approximately 30 of my colleagues and I travel to Dungarvan for a 4 day golf tournament. The jewel in the crown of our golfing year. My game plan is as follows.

On day 1, I loosen out. Day 2 is spent checking club selection, yardage etc. on each hole. Depending on my performance to the start of the round on day 3, I make my move. Day 3 is commonly known as moving day. If after 9 holes I have 20 or more stableford points, I would consolidate and play percentage golf, hoping to return a good score. A winning score at that. If my plan fails on Day 3, I would go all out on Day 4 from the start.

However, on this particular year, day 1 & 2 went according to plan and I found myself on day 3, the Wednesday, in great form and after 6 holes of play had accumulated 15 points off 12 handicap. Playing extremely well, with the help of a 'chip in' on the 8th for a birdie, had amassed 22 points after 9 holes of play. My big moment was at hand, as I started the back nine.

The wind and clouds began to gather. As I was first out that morning, by at least an hour, my thoughts were as follows. Could I reach the 18th green before the rain and wind got worse. Conditions would be very difficult for the rest of the field. All I needed was a reasonable score on the back nine. As luck would have it, I exceeded my expectations and scored 21 points. I returned a magnificent score of 43 points. I was unbeatable, Winner alright. YES SIR!!!

The wind and rain tore across from Helvick Head, over Dungarvan Bay from the Atlantic Ocean. Lovely. With a large Bushmills in hand, I sat in the bar, overlooking the course, admiring the torrential rain fall in buckets on my fellow competitors. PURE MAGIC!!!

Within the hour they crawled into the clubhouse rain sodden, dejected. I applauded each group, as they cursed the weather and thanked them for coming and contributing to the 'sweep'. It would be all mine, along with the daily winner's prize which in this case was a turkey and ham. I had no sympathy for my fellow golfers, after all, they had spent the previous night, gambling and drinking, 'till all hours and had, on more than one occasion, woke me up with their singing and door banging.

To celebrate this magnificent win, my two brothers, Bastárd, Onty and I went into town for coffee and cakes and to do the Lotto. I was alone in the shop and did my usual Lotto numbers, which were 3, 4, 12, 31, 33 and 34. Placing the ticket in my wallet, I rejoined my brothers and returned to the Gold Coast Hotel. After a swim and a sauna, we had dinner with the rest of my weather beaten friends.

Come 8PM we all started to drift back to Dungarvan to visit the imbibing emporiums. Sharing a taxi with my two brothers and me was TPO CITRUS.

Quite a few of my colleagues are amateur architects. However, they would be more interested with the interior of the imbibing emporiums than the exterior. For instance, the height of the bar stools, elbow room, the barmaid's cleavage, the colour and taste of PRAH and SENGUINS, even the texture of the whiskey. As I said before, a motley crew.

Anyway, the evening was progressing nicely, we were scattered throughout the pub. I took out my wallet and had a brief glance at my lotto ticket and asked the Bastárd to get the results of the Lotto. My wallet has been compared to the Carlsberg Complaints Department, full of cobwebs, but there is no truth in this rumour. Bastárd went to the bar to order a round and requested the lotto results. He chatted to the well endowed bar lady and returned with the drink. The lotto results were circulated among the patrons and duly arrived on our table on a large sheet of brown paper, and to my utter astonishment, I saw before me the following numbers: 3, 4, 12, 31, 33 and 37.

Retaining my composure and without batting an eyelid, I continued to sip away at my 'Mountie' club and 8UP and noticed the locals casting their eye in our direction, but thought nothing of it. After 10 minutes and unable to contain my excitement, I produced my lotto ticket and said, "Take a look at that you bastards, 5 numbers up".

Comments like, "That's great", "Fair play to yer", "Get them in" followed, but I was only half listening. I needed to know exactly how much I had won. Important decisions needed to be made. But first a urinal was needed. On the way to the gentleman's room, I mentioned my win to Timmy Cruseo and one of his drunken friends spluttered something about £1,200 for 5 numbers tonight. "Nice one", says I and added "there's a drink for all my dear golfing colleagues back at the hotel later on".

Using me computer brain with a few adjustments here and there, I arrived at a solution; £200 will be allocated for drink and £1,000 to be brought home to my dearest wife. Simple. No problem. No way.

As I returned to my table Bastárd, Onty and TPO Citrus were rubbing their hands and having a great laugh as were the rest of the patrons, at my expense, but I did not know this at the time.

'LACTURA PAUCOURM SERVA MULTOS'
'Sacrifice the few to save many'

My family motto. I also added 'TRUST NO ONE'
I ordered a round and produced a £50 note from my Carlsberg wallet. Dusting off the cobwebs, the bar lady handed back the change and winked at me. Immediately, alarm bells started going off, the word 'TRUST', for some mysterious reason, kept flashing before me. TRUST, TRUST, TRUST.

My first experience of trust happened when I was 5 years of age. My dear Papa stood me on a chair, retreated 2 paces and with outstretched arms said: "Jump Son I will catch you". I jumped into my Papa's arms but they were not there. He moved sideways and I fell onto the floor. I looked up in shock, nose bloodied and heard him say; "First lesson in life, Son, Trust no one".

On another occasion, on Christmas Eve, I was about 6 then; Papa arrived home drunk with a large brown bag. "I got yer a jigsaw puzzle" and dumped the contents on the table. It was 6d (six old pence) of broken biscuits. Trust my arse.

Needless to say the jigsaw was never completed, but the half pieces of Kimberly, Mikado and coconut cream were delicious. I never believed or trusted Santa again or Papa for that matter.

On another occasion, when Mama was in hospital, Papa asked us what we would like for dinner.

"Fish cakes" we yelled in unison.

"With or without fish" he replied. But I digress.

It was time to return to the hotel, a taxi was ordered. I was allowed to sit in the front with the driver for obvious reasons. TPO Citrus informed the driver that I had won on the Lotto. Naturally he congratulated me on my good fortune. Arriving at the hotel my 3 companions hastily alighted, leaving me to pay. From the cobweb wallet I retrieved a £5 used note. As the fare was £4, I told the taxi driver to have a week-end away on the change, on me. My generosity is only surpassed by my intellectuality and handsomeness.

Remembering the family motto 'Trust no one', I walked into the bar of the hotel and a sound of applause greeted me. Now there are times when I wouldn't be the brightest bulb on the Christmas tree, but this was not one of those occasions. I marched up to the bar and requested the barman to put RTE 1 on text mode, page 150. Silence descended on the bar. Up come page 150, Lotto results. I did not have one number.

Turning round, my 2 brothers were doubled up in laughter which in turn started every one else off, even 'Doom and Gloom' the manager. I had been truly conned.

Worse was to follow. The guys from the pub, whom I had promised a drink, returned. The explanation was given and the nicest comment I heard was, "You're a miserable billix". I tried to reason with my friends, but gave up and went to bed.

REVENGE. REVENGE IS SWEET.

I plotted my revenge. Weeks went by and I still planned. An idea formed in my mind. Then on a bleak winter's night in November, in the final year of the millennium I made a phone call to an undertaker, Mr Donovan from a public call box. "My Brother Onty has passed away"

The next morning I arrived at 79 Leopardstown Creek at 8.30 AM. My brothers, Onty and Bastárd, greeted me with the usual family theme "What do you want; we're on our way out". I brushed these comments aside and discussed the usual topics, weather etc. Golf came up and with that the con in Dungarvan. An unusual lengthy laugh followed. Then there was a knock on the door. I speedily retreated to the bathroom where I nearly pissed on myself with laughter. Of course, it was Mr Donovan, the undertaker. A verbal row ensued and I could hear many rude words been spoken. F*** off being the most prominent. The door slammed shut.

I descended the stairs of my dear brothers' home and asked what the commotion was all about. "Some billix sent an undertaker to take Onty's body away", replied Bastárd. "Dear oh dear oh dear" as a pal of mine would say.

Feigning some excuse, I quickly departed the scene. I could not bear to see their faces when the 2 skips and wedding bouquet arrived.

At the gate, the card that accompanied the wreath of Donovan Funeral Home read:

VHSG CDDODRS
RXLOZSGX
XNT
ETBJDQ

EQNL STRICHY

I put it in their letter box and ran.

N.B. An easy puzzle from the 'Da Vinci Code'

It happens between stops

John Bolton

At the time of writing I am retiring after decades working as a bus driver. Almost every journey had the makings of a story. The following is a small sample.

Christmas eve

I had to do the last bus to Ballybrack leaving at 21.00 hrs. The second last bus had only gone around the corner, when this very pregnant lady came to the door. She started her breathing exercise before she said anything. I got out and was standing beside her when she asked for Holles Street. I joked with her, that at my age I now go past it. She then asked how she would know it when she got there. I got a fright, she should not be out on her own and she should have visited it and known where it was. To break my tension I said of course you will know, there will be a bright star over head and three wise men.

Town was as dead as a dodo, only had a few on as I left at 21.00 hrs. On Merrion Square, as I got to Holles Street, I stopped in awe! There was a full moon which lit up the Square and Mount Street and just seemed to be sitting on Mount Street Bridge. When I got to the stop there were three men as drunk as Skunks in a mini scrum with a bus pole in the middle of them.

Before I opened the door to them, I told the pregnant Lady we were near Holles Street now. I told her to look up at the big moon, the bright star and look what's at the stop; your three wise men. To her credit she helped them on board. I told her to stay put and brought her to the hospital corner. I watched her go down the road and up the steps safely.

Out of curiosity, I rang Holles Street on St Stephen's day, to see what the lady had had and just to see if everything was all OK. I was asked what my relationship to her was. I stated I was not related and then the phone went dead.

"The eclipse on the cheap"

The morning news had a full load of Concorde passengers who had paid some £2,000 for a figure of eight over Tenerife to see the eclipse. This way you got to see it from both sides of the plane twice. For me, I loaded up my single decker to go to Dalkey. I got to Booterstown when I got this eerie feeling. I noticed the light change, but before I pulled back into the traffic, I noticed the start of the eclipse in the dark glass sun visor. The time was spot on between 11.18 and 11.22.

While watching this, an elderly lady asked if I was OK. I replied, "It's the eclipse, do you want to see it?"

She and all the rest queued up the centre aisle to see this from the drivers' seat. I got a great round of applause at 11.25 when it was all over.

I would be barking up the wrong tree to stick them for £2,000 each.

The guide dog

There are people in a severe state, who, I wonder how the hell they can find a Bus. The paralytic drunk gets there but I still reckon they are dumped by barmen who then run away as we come into sight. My admiration goes out to our visually impaired passengers, men like Michael Moran, who have to, "Jig Jag" through pavement works.

When he got on, a passenger asked him, "Why don't you get yourself a BLIND DOG?"

"Madam", He replied, "I have enough problems dragging this mortal coil around without having to drag that around also".

Audrey, Another of my passengers, lost her sight as a child. With the eye infection, she was able to navigate the route to school and later to university. It's only in the last two years that she got a Guide Dog.

My "Cleverest Dog" Award goes to a Man in Crumlin, who works in The Blind Factory in Rathmines. On good days, the Dog gets up at Grovner Road and rings his own bell, which hangs from his neck. He walks from there to Rathmines. On wet days, the Dog stays put until it reaches Rathmines. I should know, I saw the Dog stand up, but he didn't ring the neck bell until we got to Rathmines.

From condructress to driver

Angela Macari

A colleague showed me a video he got from a bus enthusi-
ast, who travels on his route. At first when he put it on
I thought he was showing it to me for historic interest.
There were newsreels about Dublin's transport and interesting
footage in Black and White about the role of a Bus Driver in
public transport. They looked like something you'd see in the
training School. Some news footage showed coverage of strikes
over the years and bus life changing with the times. One was
about the trouble between Dublin Bus Conductresses and a tab-
loid. Back in 1984, the very few girls working in C.I.E. varied
from married women, to school leavers. In a job mainly dominated by men, there was bound to be romances developing.

However the media got the wrong end of the stick and decided to publish an article which claimed that the behaviour of
the staff could only be compared to the soap opera 'Dallas'!

There was uproar from the clippies. They marched up to the
base of the Newspaper and demanded a retraction. I was only a
few months in C.I.E. at the time and a disillusioned school leav-
er, who was offered an application form for a job on the buses,
from the Producer of the Summerhill Garage Variety group,
also a driver. Somehow my sister and I got involved and audi-
tioned when they were putting on a show. The Variety groups
which were quite popular at the time, did 'Tops of the Town'
and many charity events too. Little did I know then, that I'd one
day be driving a bus myself!

I'm now 26 years in the Company. My circumstances and
home address changed a few times but I remained faithful to
my job and it has given me lots of friends, hobbies and a secure
income. I've never regretted a day.

My colleague was particularly excited when the story came
up about 'The Sunday World' row in 1984. A shot of Donnybrook Garage and its busy forecourt came into view. Then the

camera zoomed in on four conductresses chatting as they came out of the depot. My friend asked did I recognise any of them. I only recognised two. He asked about the girl in the middle and there was something familiar about her. It was me twenty years younger!

Memories came flooding back about the way life was for me then. I remembered being warned that the hours would be unsociable. The uniforms were only available in men's sizes and certainly didn't allow for curvaceous ladies. This pretty much showed the dim forecast the company had for our survival. We were despised by senior men, but tolerated by the randy young men who fancied the idea of a woman in a blue uniform. This wasn't as nice as it sounds. When you are knackered after rising at five A.M. and walking up and down a bus saying 'Fares please!' climbing stairs and inhaling cigarette smoke, the advances of the driver is only another headache.

To put up the destination involved climbing onto the tin box which encased the ticket machine, turning handles that were rusted or covered with grease and usually breaking a fingernail or grazing your skin.

A typical day on an early week for me started with getting up at five, to get the workman bus at five fifty up on the South Circular Road. I usually had two choices. Press snooze or have breakfast. Snooze won! Thus my lovely svelte figure in the video!

At the garage I'd run upstairs to the canteen to get a coffee from the vending machine, go up for the running board, grab a waybill and get my machine from my locker. You loaded your tin box with bus rolls and then you'd head out to meet your driver with the bus. I got on with most of the drivers even though they often asked me to pipe down. I was very chatty!

My social life was curtailed too. I was still in the Variety group so on breaks in the evening I often headed upstairs in the Bus Canteen in Earl Place, to rehearse after doing a part pay in at the cash office and then I'd have my packed lunch and a coke during the rehearsal. Those were fun times. I remember on one occasion when I went in to have a shot at the snooker. The driver I was with was a dab hand at it. He gave me a shot and as I stretched across to take it, a ripping sound made us stop. It was my trousers which had ripped on the inside leg!

The gape was major and the idea of walking the decks of a bus with most of my thigh on show wasn't nice, so I ran across to the uniform stores and fortunately got a replacement pair in time to get back to my bus for the second half of the duty.

Looking back at times like this makes me feel old. But there have been so many changes over the years. Bus conductors are now extinct. There are new routes, a variety of cultures and nationalities among the staff and even the City we drive across has altered enormously.

In 2008 I received a commemorative watch for my twenty five years service to Dublin Bus along with people I was in the training school with. When I look at the photograph taken on that happy occasion, it is all the reward I need and proves that the job I came into twenty five years ago, has grown and improved. Let's hope it never stops!

A BULL FOR BINGHAMSTOWN

Joe Collins

The sun was shining brightly on that Saturday afternoon in August 1955. It was the start of the Bank Holiday weekend and I, like everybody else, was hoping for a pleasant break from work.

At the time I was a Junior Clerical Officer employed by Coras Iompair Eireann in Limerick and as the 5 day week had not yet come into being I was working that afternoon from 2 PM. to 6 PM to complete my $5^{1/2}$ day week.

At 5 PM as I was winding down the Livestock loading porter and another man entered the office and the porter said, "Sir we have a Bull for Binghamstown".

"Binghamstown" I said, "where is that"? The man who accompanied the porter said

"it is in Mayo way beyond Belmullet. Before dealing with the Bull's journey let me give you some information on the Bull."

He was owned by the Dept of Agriculture and was part of what was known as the Travelling Bull Scheme. He was in fact one of a group of Roaming Romeos who at that time traversed the country to increase the bovine population.

In 1956 Artificial Insemination had not yet been in general usage and the natural method of procreation was still in full swing as was their Eco Friendliness by their use of Public Transport.

As I pondered how I was going to tackle the problems associated with the transport of a bull over a Bank Holiday Weekend from Limerick to Binghamstown I could not understand why the bull's next performance was not in Tipperary or some other venue closer to Limerick. I was reminded of the crazy schedules of the Dance Bands at that time; any of which in the course of their 6 day work week

Tuesday through Sunday would criss cross the country playing Letterkenny, Limerick, Dundalk, Dingle, Westport and Waterford in that or some similar madcap geographic spread...

But back to the Bull. Throughout his Marathon Journey he needed to be fed and watered and the bedding in the Cattle Truck had to be replaced and the dung removed. The various train drivers and train guards on the journey had to ensure that there was no rough shunting, in fact nothing could be done that would damage his masculinity.

Now in 1955 there were no faxes, telexes, emails or mobile phones and the telephone system in operation was primitive. Before this bull could leave Limerick I had to make contact with Ballybrophy Station and North Wall Dublin to put the arrangements in train for his safe passage. Ballybrophy was not too difficult as being a station on the Dublin-Cork Mainline with an active signal cabin I got a quick response. The Station Master came on the line and having explained about the bull's needs he assured me that at his station all the necessary feeding, watering and cleaning would be done. After all said he, "I have a family connection with farming and know the importance of pampering these premium bulls to ensure fertile performance".

At North Wall I was not so lucky. Firstly making contact was most difficult and when I did the person at the other end of the phone was most unsympathetic to the bull in transit. After an outburst of expletives and a tirade of abuse for daring to land him with this problem at such a late hour on the Saturday of a Bank Holiday Weekend when as he said he should be knocking back pints he went on to issue threats of what he wouldn't do to the bull including making him fit only for Guard Duty in a Bovine Harem if he failed to get a colleague to come on duty in the early hours of Sunday morning to deal with the bull's needs.

Regarding the arrangements to be made beyond North Wall he would not get involved and left it up to me to sort that out. Luckily I had no difficulty at the intermediate stations as those to whom I spoke were of similar mind to the Station Master at Ballybrophy. They were all men with an affinity to farming and they appreciated the value of the contribution of farming to the local economy.

My final obstacle was encountered at Ballina. Here the onward journey by road had to be arranged. Unfortunately the Station Master was on leave and was replaced by a Relief Clerk who like the Bulls in the Travelling Bull Scheme belonged to a group of Travelling Gap Fillers drafted in to Stations in the event of Illness or Annual Leave of the resident staff.

On explaining to the Relief Clerk about the arrangements he had to make for the final leg of the journey from Ballina to Binghamstown he feigned ignorance of the names of local lorry drivers who provided services to C.I.E. from time to time on a contractual basis saying that it was his first time relieving in Ballina and he could not help. He was he said more interested in getting ready for the local hop where he might meet a Juliet than worrying about the Bovine Romeo en route to Binghamstown.

While pleading with him to assist he hung up on me and despite my efforts to re-establish contact I failed.

At my wits end I phoned the local Garda Station and asked if they could provide the names of a few lorry owners who transported livestock and to their credit they came up trumps.

Lady Luck smiled on me as the first call I made produced a willing carrier to transport Romeo to his Juliet in Binghamstown. Because the trip would be undertaken on Sunday the carrier requested a premium payment to which I agreed even though I did not have the authority to do so and would likely have to pay the excess from my own pocket when the bill arrived. But I felt that the loss of a few pounds was nothing compared to the contribution I was making to facilitate the romantic meeting of the Travelling Tarbh and the Binghamstown Beauty.

I never heard anything about the excess payment or if the Romantic Union produced an Issue. However the odds are that there are descendants of the Travelling Romeo and the Bellingham Beauty alive and well in Ireland today oblivious to the Herculean efforts of a Junior Clerical Officer employed by C.I.E.in Limerick to bring their ancestors together on a Sunny Bank Holiday Weekend in August 1955.

DONNYBROOK MAINTENANCE IN THE 80'S

Pat Barrett

This is the story of an operative in Donnybrook in the 80's; Joe Maguire, a man in his late fifties and true blue Dubliner. He had worked for the company for many years as a labourer in Spa Road and later as a cleaner in Donnybrook. He was a quiet man who went about his business largely unnoticed by many except those who worked in proximity to him. A man of obvious habit who could be seen every day at four thirty (finishing time in maintenance) on his loping half canter and half run down the centre yard and up Eglinton road.

Most people were only aware of him when he went around the various canteens, gathering up discarded sandwiches and bread and breaking it up into small pieces and placing it into a small plastic bag he carried. Joe was of the old stock and wore the same clean but faded overalls for many years. This combined with the Brylcreamed hair, stuck to his head gave him the look of someone from a different era.

My story is set in the context of his habits of gathering the bread and distributing it to the flocks of seagulls that gathered around and above him as soon as he emerged from the workshop into the centre yard. It was a sight to behold to see him throwing handfuls of bread into the air, whilst urging the birds to be patient and "wait their turn".

Of course the inevitable happened and the birds would shit on anything that moved after their constant and handsome meals. This was never considered a major problem, until, they followed him inside into the large garage area. Their defecating seemed to increase when inside and caused problems for the men working there. The result of this caused untold discomfort and the "unions" were informed and asked the manager to get it sorted.

The garage manager naturally devolved responsibility to the foreman to tell Joe to "stop feeding those fucking things and drawing them inside".The foreman whose name was Charlie, told Joe, " if I catch you feeding them again I will sack you". To the foreman this of course ensured Joe would cease the practise and the problem would go quietly away. However, this was not to be.

About a week later, very early in the morning the foreman and I were working away in the office (the office overlooked the bus pits). I happened to look down onto the shop floor and noticed Joe, walking along the top of the pits and about six or seven pigeons were walking with him. I asked Charlie did he not say anything to Joe and showed him what was happening. Charlie jumped up from his chair and with anger as his mask, left the office. I could see him pursuing Joe with increasing speed, but, to my surprise Charlie stopped short and after a moment turned and returned to my office. When he arrived he was laughing and when asked, "why didn't you say anything to Joe"? he replied " just as I got close to Joe I noticed he was making hand gestures and I heard him say to the pigeons ' get up, get up for fuck sake, here's Charlie'".

THE REPAIR JOB

Thomas Carroll

Kevin sat up in the bed his wounds almost healed, the-bandages still bloody were hurting his hands and arms;he could see bloodstains on the bed sheets. What's the use in having a dog his mother always said if you have to do the barking? That's how he felt now; deep down in his mind the events of the past nine days were played out in vivid detail. He could still see the hulking figure of O'Regan otherwise known as **Conan the Terrible** chasing him down the narrow streets of Turin; bullets' ricocheting off high stonewalls, innocent people being shot up in the fierce crossfire. Kevin's cover had been blown by a stupid mistake on the part of his now dead partner, Miles Murphy. Kevin and Miles were posing as plumbers trying to repair a leaking shower unit in an expensive Italian mafia gang-lord's villa. Their real function was to take out this hardened criminal preferably alive. But due to the sloppiness of Miles Ryan and the fact that he completely busted the shower unit both men were given a hasty exit. Luckily Kevin managed to escape with his life. But only just.

How am I ever going to rectify this situation thought Kevin as he stared at his bandaged hands and arms? I won't be ready for action for at least two months and by that time O' Regan will be a criminal of the distant past. Just then Nurse Michel entered the room. She was preparing to give Kevin a bed-bath which as far as he was concerned was the only nice thing about being in hospital (at least for some people). She smelled of expensive perfume so Kevin did the natural thing and began to compliment her on her choice of fragrance. "Armani or Lautrec?" Kevin asked with a deliberate smile. "Lautrec of course. It's guaranteed to hit all the right notes for a man," Nurse Michel said as she began scrubbing Kevin's feet. In eight weeks Kevin had recovered; he was a healthy, fit man and his wounds healed fast. Also the extensive treatment worked wonders for his injured arms.

He wouldn't have a partner for the remainder of this assignment because the department were a little short staffed and anyway with so many trouble spots throughout the world they couldn't afford to spare a single agent. So Kevin would go on the mission alone. "This envelope contains all the necessary papers that will ensure your speedy entry into Yugoslavia," said Major Malone handing Kevin a large brown Manila envelope. "Best be on your way there's a car waiting outside to take you to the airport. Your flight's in three hours. Best of luck captain," said the major as the two men got to their feet and shookhands. The major knew the chances of Kevin being successful in this operation were slim indeed; but the major did not reveal this thought. Anyone facing a difficult situation needs reassuring, that's what the army manual stated and that's what the major tried to convey in his voice and handshake.

It was a bad, wet night; the rain pounding off the road made an impenetrable spray. Kevin, drenched to the bone clutched his Mauser pistol; he hoped that it would still discharge the last 24 rounds of ammunition. If it failed he might find himself a dead man and that negative outcome just would not do. Kevin found his target and the bullet pierced his assailant's head, the man dropped dead to the ground. Kevin grabbed the man's automatic and his hand gun, he had a feeling he would need the weapons. Suddenly bullets exploded around him; scrambling for cover he dived behind some laundry containers. Barrels and other items exploded and shattered; automatic fire was coming from his left. He could see three men firing from behind a parked car. Kevin would have to use all his training to get out of this predicament. In the midst of all this mayhem Kevin remembered a line from the SAS Survival Manual: *When you are faced with difficult situations always breathe deeply and calmly so as to fill your brain and your body with oxygen which in turn will ensure your mind thinks clearly and positively. Hence the outcome of your situation will be 99.9% successful.* It's the undetermined 0.1% that worries me thought Kevin. The SAS instructors had always taught that an agent must use all his resources even when reduced to a broken man or woman. *"He Who Dares Wins"* – that was the famous motto and a principle that Kevin and many other agents were taught to live and if necessary, to die by. Kevin killed the three bodyguards and made his entry into O'Regan's penthouse hotel suite. Carefully he opened the door and fired a round at O'Regan who yelped in pain as his automatic weapon blew out of his hand. O'Regan fell to the floor, blood pouring from his hand. Kevin ran into the room, knelt down and clamped his right foot on O'Regan's good hand.

"Why should I care what happens to your dirty henchmen; you are after all a bunch of criminals" said Kevin pointing the gun at O'Regan.

"Come and work for me. You will be better paid and will be able to buy whatever riches you want in life," O' Regan said with a wry smile. Kevin's gun was pressing against his chest.

"That would be a mistake I might never live to regret," Kevin said staring into O'Regan's black pupils. In those milliseconds Kevin's mind replayed the incidents which led to his partner Miles Murphy's death. *The awful figure of O'Regan loomed ever closer; his big shovel-like hands clutching the Kalashnikov machine gun. He rounded a corner in Bratislava Street close to the bullet-ridden car where Miles Murphy lay dead. O' Regan's men had already seen to Murphy's demise. Kevin continued to run ahead of the big man conscious of the closing gap.* Now in this very moment big, warm drops of sweat formed on Kevin's forehead; the gun feeling slippery in his hand, he had to persist. Pressing the gun harder into O' Regan's chest Kevin knew he could win this battle. He might not win the war but he might just terminate O'Regan and vindicate Miles Murphy's death.

"Do you think I care? You are nothing but a loser. You have traded the food of the gods for a mess of pottage", the big man just smirked."Go ahead and pull the trigger; bet you haven't the balls to do it?"

Just then the door of the room burst open, it was Ray Sullivan and three other members of the SAS swat team. They stormed into the room and surrounded Kevin and O'Regan.

"He's dangerous Ray he's a cold blooded killer," Kevin said still pressing his gun into O'Regan. 'I should've blown the bastard away while I had a chance'. "Easy Kevin; we want this fish alive; that way he's more useful to us. He's got more information about the plot to smuggle nuclear warheads than any person alive on the planet," Ray said slightly angling his automatic at Kevin. It was then that Kevin realised that he was being double crossed by his own SAS regiment.

Kevin got off of O'Regan's chest. His gun still pointed at the big man on the floor.

"Why are you doing this," asked Kevin. "Not alone are you lot betraying your country you're betraying everything the SAS stands for."

"It's complicated Kevin. The plot's pretty involved. I think we should go somewhere, the two of us, and I could explain it to you."

"I just bet you could."

"Huh?"

There was a loud scream as O'Regan lunged head first at Ray. The force of the attack knocked Ray to the floor. His gun went off, bullets striking two of the swat team who fell to the floor like mown down weeds. Kevin dived behind a large leather sofa as O'Regan grabbed the fallen weapon and sprayed the room with automatic gun fire. One of the remaining SAS swat team managed to return fire before being shot to bits. Kevin carefully aimed his final two shots at the hulking figure of O'Regan who now had his back to the large window.

"See you in hell!" shouted O' Regan as he prepared to unleash copious amounts of lead into the leather sofa.

Kevin pressed the trigger, the bullet caught O'Regan right in the forehead, the force of which blew him out the window and the second shot drove him somersaulting over the small balcony wall.

Kevin raced to the shattered window and looking out over the tiny balcony he saw O'Regan lying dead on the pavement below; a crowd of shocked people already gathering. Night had fallen, the torrential rain had ceased; a silver and white full moon illuminated the starry night sky.

Kevin walked into the wrecked room and having ascertained that all three of the SAS swat team were dead made sure to administer first aid to Ray who was more injured by O'Regan's head butting than anything else. Kevin then handcuffed Ray. As the police arrived and Ray Sullivan was led away Kevin realized with relief that he had at last accomplished his mission.

Kevin settled into his seat on the airplane and for the first time in his life he felt really relaxed and promptly fell asleep. A few hours later having arrived back in Washington Kevin entered the top level security of the Pentagon to brief Major Malone on the whole messy business. When he had finished he looked the major in the eye and said 'This is one repair job I want to forget!'

"You can take it from me captain that all the gory details will be carefully concealed. The details of sensitive missions are never revealed to the media. What is said in this room is strictly between you and me," the major said, his decorated uniform sparkling in the spring sunlight which shone through the large bay windows. Kevin noticed that the major's uniform showed he had been decorated at least twelve times which meant that he must have been a damned good agent in his day.

"And by the way you deserve a holiday. Here is a return ticket to the Bahamas. Enjoy your vacation," the major said. "I intend to," said a delighted and smiling Kevin as he took the tickets from the major.

"Oh just one last thing Major I never again want an assignment that involves posing as a repair man. After all I and many of your field agents are not trained as plumbers or mechanics; a repair job has the potential to become a complete mess. We are however trained as professional soldiers and mercenaries."

"Point taken; see you in six weeks time," Major Malone said, his lips thin and his face impassive. When Kevin had left the room Major Malone put a hand underneath his desk and switched off the digital recording device. The soundtrack of their conversation would be stored away in a high security vault deep within the chasms of the Pentagon and if Major Malone ever thought that an agent would be corrupted in any way he wouldn't hesitate to make use of these recordings. Major Malone smiling leaned back in his high leather chair and thought to himself *I am the main man in this outfit and I always win in any repair job.*

SUNDRIVE PARK

Ronnie Hickey

Green and gold
In amber sunlight
Dogs bark
And children screech
Along the paths
By blossoming trees.

They will never know
That this was once
A watery grave
Where unloved cats and dogs
Ended their earthly span
Amid the silent screams
Of boys and girls
Sinking under
The winter's ice,
A bottomless pit,
It was said,
Never to be seen again.

We view the city's sunlit spires
Green domes and shiny roofs,
Remembering.
Molling through the tip head
Resurrecting cinders
To keep the home fires burning
At sixpence a bag.

By daylight,
We watch young couples
Embracing under an open sky
Where long ago
Surreptitious lovers
Nightly shared
Forbidden secrets
Mouth to mouth
And shed their fruits
Darkly along the
Rat infested banks.

We must ask,
Should children now
Be burdened with
Our faded past.
Children in
A bright new world
Assembling joys
On soccer pitches
Running tracks
Reaching through the shadows
Of drugs and drink
And the savagery
Of a world
Searching for old ways
Free of jaded mythologies.

THE GREEN MACHINE

Jimmy Curran

If I said, Giovanni Riccardi, you might think of an Italian restaurant owner or, a first cousin to the Sopranos. Well he is none of the above and he doesn't own a chipper in Ballyfermot. Giovanni Riccardi or "Gio" as he known is an Italian bus driver in Phibsboro bus garage in Dublin. He is married with one son and lives in Clondalkin, Dublin. He came from Naples fifteen years ago and worked at many jobs from driving to trying his hands doing what Italians do best frying chips in a mobile chip van. The mobile chip van was made and fitted by "Gio".

A big task to make something like that, this is where his skills as a fitter went into action. He made a living out of this for some time until he discovered that two of his employees were ripping him off and sharing his profits. Gio served his time as a fitter back home in Italy. Times were hard and he worked for nothing at times for the experience. He also gained a very wide knowledge of motor mechanics and body work on cars and never gives up when he starts a project.

Gio has restored many cars from what was a piece of junk to be a pristine showroom work of art. I have seen film footage of his work and with his skill, he has no fear of a job and hard work is the order of the day. So when I first noticed his 1992 Nissan Sunny before I knew the person who owned this car it got my attention. The body work is totally unblemished and looking into the interior you soon know the person that owns this car has pride in it.

This is how I got to talk to "Gio" about this car. One day he was standing in the yard in Phibsboro bus garage the car engine was running as we chatted.

I could not help notice the smell coming from the exhaust of his car as it ticked over, it was a smell of chips cooking. So being a cheeky Irish man I asked the Italian what was the smell.

He laughed a little before telling me his 1.8 diesel engine was running on used cooking oil. At this point he had me laughing with him. As I have a big interest in cars it was time for "Gio" to do a little explaining.

He makes a weekly trip to a well known chipper in Dublin where he picks up 10 maybe 20 litres of used cooking oil from the owner. Normally the owner has to pay a company to come and collect and dispose of this oil in the interest of the environment. When the oil arrives in "Gio's" garage it is placed into a tank which contains a filter where it passes through this filter and into another filter before entering a drum under the bench.

The oil is removed via a tap and it is put into a container and then into his fuel tank in his car. This refining system requires no power and is run on gravity another contribution to the environment.

So far this story is not Arab friendly.

From the time this oil left the chipper it has been filtered twice and as an added security "Gio" has put an additional fuel filter within the car as the Kerry man says, to be sure to be sure, the oil is filtered twice under the bonnet before being injected into the engine.

In the early days of this venture he was going into the unknown so he started by mixing the cooking oil with diesel on a 50/50 basis. He reduced it over a 14 day period getting it down to pure unused cooking oil. In another experiment "Gio" decided to get himself down to his local Chinese wholesaler and purchase 20litres of pure unused cooking oil thinking the car would run even better. To his disappointment the car would not run at all, reason being this oil was rice oil and not sunflower oil, he now knows that his engine dos not run on Chinese rice oil.

All went well for some time until driving home one evening the car began to slow down to a crawl. After getting home he stripped down the fuel pump to discover it was totally seized.

It was his opinion because of the density of pure undiluted oil the pump was working twice as hard as it normally would to pump this oil. This did not deter this determent Italian who got himself off to the breaker's yard and got himself another pump fitted it, and away again.

At this point not wanting to use any chemicals he decided to step back again and mix 50/50 with diesel and decrease the density of the fuel and take the pressure of the fuel pump.

The original pump, having being taken from the car, was immersed in a container of paraffin and low and behold yes its spanking brand new again and is on standby.

On a recent visit to the N.C.T.Centre "Gio" watched as the mechanic took his car off one fuel emissions machine and try it on another as he could not understand the reading he was getting. The reading was 0.02/m almost nil emissions. This was much to Gio's amusement.

The staff at the testing centre were quite amazed to find that the car was running on used cooking oil. This experiment has not been easy from the beginning it was a risk that Gio took with confidence. It involved his expertise to be put to the ultimate test. It meant getting dirty a lot of the time.

As he spends a lot of time collecting this oil and refining it through his system he feels that out there somebody in the science field has the answer to his home refining. But it is in the interest of the environment, that this whole project started from. For that reason, he feels that introducing chemicals would forego the whole idea, and not contribute to the environment.

It is his opinion that the motor industry is not really interested in bio fuels and fails to make a positive effort to come up with the answers for a simple project like Gio's.

He has run experiments with a central heating burner with this fuel, and has run the unit on used cooking oil. He has also run his car on used engine oil that had come from his car after an oil change. Once a fuel is combustible he believes that it has a purpose and can be used if the right adjustments are made.

On the down side of the experiment because of the home-made refining the car will use oil filters a lot quicker than the ordinary car, this is something that Gio is working on at present and is conducting daily experiments on the car on his journeys from Clondalkin to Phibsboro garage.

Finally Gio is prepared to offer to let any person take his car without notice to be tested or examined in any way to prove all the above. At the end of the day Gio is making a very big saving over his yearly fuel bill, with this car, and he makes this car work for him like a horse drawing a trailer at times carrying a lot of weight for his metal skills in making gates and railings. This car is running better now than it did six years ago when he first got it. It has paid for itself in more ways than one.

Gio is also self sufficient in home-heating fuel; heating his home entirely from wood, which he collects with his car and trailer, and nothing else through a back boiler system heating the radiators in his home. Not bad for an Italian living in Ireland who looks about the same height as Frankie Detorri and would not look out of place in Fairy House on Grand National day in cap and colours.

So the next time you are in the chipper getting your "one and one" remember Gio could be waiting out the back with his barrel doing his bit for the environment and saving money.

ANTHROPAMORPHIZE

Mark Bolger

Dave reached across the table, "Listen you're going to make me a cup of tea whether you want to or not!" His comment was answered with a hiss. Sibilant and throaty.

He watched as a bead of wet ran down her sleek figure, and caught himself from extending his hand to stop its progress. The silence in the room stretched time until it seemed it could snap, a thousand ticks suddenly in search of finding their elusive counterpart; the tock. Sending the world into the chaos of boulders rolling up hills and the sun rising at night and setting in the morning. He shook off the mental image of a world of fractured time, knowing that unless he stopped now, he would pursue it obsessively.

He also knew better than to touch her at times like this, knowing full well that she would more likely than not, do damage to his digits.

He sighed; the need for that cup of tea had left him, along with his masculinity. Shoulders slumped he made his way into the living room. Looking back once he could see that she hadn't moved, not that he really expected her too. He couldn't help but focus on her lip, stuck out in an almost perpetual pout. He knew that any warmth passing that pout now would be bitter and caustic, untrue.

Or maybe that is how he would perceive it. The end result is the same regardless; Perception is in the eye of the beholder he thought, smiling to himself, knowing she would never get the subtleties that that comment was laden with.

Secretly pleased with his own wit and cleverness he left the room, his inner comment boosting his ego back up to its normal sybaritic levels.

"Who needs tea anyway?" he said just loud enough for it to carry back into the kitchen.

"I know I don't. Sure I can always have a glass of coke if I'm thirsty."

Dave knew that that last jibe was beneath him, but he was also aware that the human spirit needed a little regress back to juvenility if only to make it appreciate more when it was forced to be all adult and serious. "So looks like it's just me and you tonight," Dave said across the room to his friend.

His friend started singing a well-known ditty about sanitary pads. Dave wondered if she would be able to hear if body form was for her from the kitchen. Laughing, he picked up the remote and TV guide and flopped back into one of the sofas directly across from his friend.

"Nail on the head good buddy. You called that right."

His friend was already rambling on about what was on a particular channel that night, it was the usual mix of reality shows and celebrities struggling to claw back their heyday fame.

"They should do a show, where Z-list celebrities are all locked up in a house together on a deserted island, with old animals that they perform surgery on and then train to fix up and decorate a living room. Using only tat that the animals themselves have bought at a car boot sale under the advisement of an effeminate expert on all things naff. The trainers of the two winning animals then have to go on a blind date together and that segment can be peppered with idiotic monologues of them both trying out their pop psychology on what makes the other tick and how in their opinion the other would be doing themselves a favour if only they could learn to play down that annoying habit that has obviously surfaced due to some Freudian episode from the annals of their childhood and if they were a more self aware person like the more enlightened of us are, they would see it and take steps to remedy these particular character flaws. That would free up the schedule listings so they can go back to basics and actually have some decent programming."

He looked up from the TV guide to see how well received his imagined show montage might be. His friend was talking about what the weather was going to be like over the next three days. Jees, all that effort for nothing, he thought, but still a bit pleased with himself for his little caustic rhetoric.

"It'll be sunny, with patches of rain throughout the day tomorrow..."

Dave loved his friend, but his attention span left a lot to be desired. He had an awful tendency to chatter on about the most inane things. However at the same time he could make Dave laugh or cry. No mean feat. He didn't know anyone else who could have that dichotomy of effects on him. In a few short sentences he could instil in Dave such a sense of wonder about the world, and then ten minutes later a crushing sense of guilt.

Still, it's nice to have a friend you can always rely on, he thought. Someone who didn't judge, and always lent a kind ear. Settling back he flicked through the channels until he found the one he wanted. A movie about someone good-looking kicking a lot of baddies butts was just starting. Just what the night called for, chewing gum for the mind. He needed something to help him switch off; the broken time idea kept jumping back into his head. An unwelcome visitor; the person you meet on holidays and insincerely offer to put up if they are ever in your neck of the woods, knowing and hoping a little that they will never take you up on your offer.

It had, despite actively trying to avoid it, quickly gotten to the point that he kept imagining that everything he did was backwards or out of sequence. His inner child had even pictured him wiping the back of his jeans with toilet paper before pulling his pants down and experiencing a sudden bloated feeling as a rather large faeces jumped from the bowl into his colon, or other equally strange versions. Then he would find himself outside the door of the bathroom wearing a grimace and wondering why he felt the need to undress to go to work.

When ideas like this took hold of his thoughts he wondered not for the first time if he was actually mad.

Trying to ignore them, they kept crawling insidiously back into his conscious mind, they become the tooth with the missing filling that no matter how hard you try you cannot seem to stop your tongue from prodding and probing until the jagged edges have left their mark, dozens of little tongue lacerations that proved once again that you should have stopped before you started. He had on a few occasions tried surreptitiously to question friends and family to see if they had similar thoughts, but he had always come up short of an answer. The working theory so far was that they did in fact have the same, if not worse, thoughts as him but were also as confused as he was, and like him failed to be as honest as he wished the rest of the world should be. So believing they are less than sane they kept their mental misgivings to themselves for fear that they were wrong and the world would see them for the nutters they were.

He also sometimes imagined it would be fun in a mental institution; there would be an enormously liberating sense of freedom that you were no longer beholden to society's mores. You could pick your nose in public, swear at the top of your voice, dance naked to an imagined song with that sense of freedom from embarrassment that only the very young have. Before they too are programmed by society as to what is or is not acceptable.

In fact all round he guessed that an institute seems like a very sweet deal indeed. Three square meals a day, more happy pills than you could ever need and maybe even the occasional blanket bath from a pretty nurse dressed in pristine starched whites. However it was freedom that kept him from exploring that particular path. Freedom to have a cup of tea when he chose. Freedom to watch TV when he felt like it, and to watch what he wanted and not have his viewing screened, monitored and chosen for him. Real freedom, not imagined. Forget the nuthouse he told himself.

The movie ran its course to its predictable ending and Dave felt thankful for its empty content. It was fun to just sit in silence every now and then, without the head doing what it normally did and making more out of things than they had any right to be. Switching the movie off and saying goodnight to his friend at the door he looked toward the kitchen door knowing that behind it she had spent the night sulking. Slightly guilty he looked up the hall and with a knowing nod to his friend quietly closed the door and crept upstairs. The upstairs landing posed another dilemma when indecision and a slight sense of guilt grabbed him, cursing himself for being so caught up in others, Dave took a deep breath. Knowing she would spend the night downstairs he ignored the voice in his head and headed toward the spare room whilst consciously ignoring the fact that he was passing his own room.

The spare room door opened with a slight creak.

'That looks comfy. Can I come in?' he spoke a darkly whisper into the shadowy room.

Creeping across the beige carpet he quickly shed his clothes dropping them in an untidy pile on the floor and slid under the covers.

Reaching his hand across the bed he caressed and held, content. With pillows softness he spooned and quickly fell asleep to dream dreams of friends, crowds and laughter.

Waking early the next morning he got up quickly and quietly. Then looked down at the bed with its crumpled memories and a slight remorse, the telltale lump of his presence morphed into an accusing finger pointing at him; he picked up his previously discarded clothes and fled naked from the room.

When he entered the kitchen it seemed to be as silent as it had the night before. Stretching across the counter he switched on the radio, the smooth false voice of the faceless DJ filled the room promising some lucky listener a chance to win two tickets to a day spa filled the room. All they had to do was get on air and embarrass themselves vocally to the ears of thousands of listeners.

The background noise of the radio seemed to warm the space a little, adding aural colour to the pots, pans and appliances.

Looking over she still wore the same pout as she had the night before, inwardly Dave sighed, and he could feel that she was cold towards him this morning too. Bloody hell it seemed like she was cold every morning now. He had hoped that the silliness of last night would be over, it seemed that it wasn't. Guess I'll have to be the bigger man, he thought.

"Morning Hun, how are you today?" he asked, not expecting a reply.

Ignoring the silence, "Well I'm fine, thanks for asking." he continued talking as if both were having the conversation. "Hmm, a cup of coffee would be lovely about now. Wake me up. Don't you think?"

Dave reached out, picked up the Kettle and filled it from the tap. Switching it on he started gathering together the bits and bobs necessary for a cuppa. Milk, coffee, sugar, spoon etc. Looking back at her he saw that she had started to warm up.

About time, he thought.

Out loud. "Yep. I think it's going to be a nice day. Don't you?"

He picked up the kettle and began pouring. Distracted, waiting for an answer to his query, his attention was drawn away from what he was doing.

Suddenly a sharp, liquid scream ran up the nerves of his left hand, this message - help I'm being cooked - was a slow second to his dropping the cup and even slower third to slamming the kettle down on the counter top to free that hand to nurse the scalded other.

The dropped cup threw out a hot fan of pain across Dave's torso. Sprinkled stings combined in a synergy of agony. Visions of skin grafts and blisters hit his mind like a lightning flash view, instant and fleeting.

"Shit! Shit! Shit!.. You mother fu... Aaaaoooowwwcchhh!!!"

Storming over to the other side of the kitchen Dave glared back at her whilst clutching his clawed left hand to his freshly burned chest with his sympathetic right.

" You... did... that... on purpose! You BITCH!" he screamed.

The scream, the pain and the moment all seemed to gel and clarify that instant.

He realised what had been happening. How he was being made a fool of. In fact, how he was making a fool of himself. Moments of happiness slipped through his mind, memories laughing on the sofa, washing dishes, sitting bolt upright from a dream with a smile. God how could he have been so stupid, how had he let things get this far.

Taking a deep breath he stood straight, faced her while still clutching his injured hand, and said, "I realise that this situation cannot go on any longer..." a deep breath, calming himself, bracing for the truth, the obvious, the necessary.

"In fact it seems to me that it's nuts, it's no good for me and as you can see it is actually causing harm." He waved his burnt and scalded hand to emphasise this point.

"Besides..." he continued, feeling nasty. "You're nothing but..." he paused for effect and to wonder if he should admit it...

"A FUCKING KETTLE! A KITCHEN APPLIANCE! Why do I even give you my time?"

He stormed out of the kitchen slamming the door behind him. Leaving the kettle sat on the worktop amidst the cooling liquid shrapnel.

In the living room he sat down heavily on the sofa holding his wounded limb with a care normally reserved for mothers and nurses. Across the room his friend sat quietly in the corner.

"I guess you've heard..." he pointed his injured hand toward his friend emulating a wince to show the pain he was in. "So what do you think?" he asked.

His friend sat silent, still, waiting.

"What am I asking you for?" The television, his supposed friend, sat oblivious to this new drama unfolding, its dead grey eye looked upon the room with a complete lack of caring, a reflection of the sitting room stretched fish eyed across the screen. Showing the room with its armchairs, bad wallpaper and only Dave, sat clutching his arm close while looking at the floor with a haunted, worried look on his face.

Imagining the bed upstairs in the spare room having a good laugh at his expense from all of his romantic gestures and pillow talk was all he could take. Slowly putting his face into his hands the sobs began. With elbows on knees a slow keening began to issue from him, each sob breaking the constancy of this quiet wail. With understanding the pain eventually became a full-blown cry, the choking blubbers catching themselves, until only a hiccupped broken silence was all that remained to fill the room.

When you are a child with a new pair of runners you are convinced that they can make you run faster. What happens when you realise that you were wrong all along? Do you stop even trying to run? Or does disappointment crush you and all your hopes so even walking seems an effort?

The rocking began and hands slid down from the face to clutch around his body in an attempt to stop from coming apart.

'Am I mad?' His head screamed at him.

The silence of an empty house screamed back.

MR. MACTIGHT

Thomas Carroll

M r MacTight sat at his desk till all hours of the night writing diddly, fiddly doodles which were usually misspelt and if these ditties were vocalised they would sound like a walrus belching while trying to clamber onto the rocks which adjoined the beach at Ballyheigue, County Kerry. But if there was one thing which Mr MacTight always got right it was his love of growing plants and pottering about in his glass house; in rain and shine you would see him with his orange wellies carrying container plants in and out of the glass house. But sometimes during a very wet summer more than likely he'd be shovelling muck and cursing the rain as it washed his garden soil clean away and with all the recent flooding his garden had now become a lake!

In no time at all ducks and fish and seals and otters moved in to Mr MacTight's flooded garden. The poor man felt like drowning himself; he was at his wits end! What could he do? Then he remembered a self-help CD by Anthony Robbins called 'Master Your Time'. If this could not help he didn't know what he would do!

So each day he would listen to the CD and try to implement all the good sound advice contained therein. But alas Mr Mac-Tight realised he had lived a very bad life indeed! What with his predilection for the cursed 'drink' and chasing young comely maidens about town and further afield too, his life he now could see quite clearly was a big fat lie! Self-deception was indeed very cruel when he confronted himself in the damp stained mirror which hung in his bathroom wall.

Which is all the more reason why portly Mr MacTight opted to live with the pigs in the pigsty! At least that way he would never feel above his own station in life. So now every day he grovelled and rolled around in the mud quite happy along with all the pigs!

When last anyone saw or heard of Mr MacTight it was reported by the local gossip merchants he had sold up and gone on retreat to live with Tibetan monks in Ulan Bater situated in Outer Mongolia. Some say he mentioned that the move would help him find his 'true-self'. The only correspondence that ever appeared after he had been gone for more than five years was this hand printed sentence on the back of a post card with a Tibetan stamp:

'*You must be the change you wish to see in the world.*'
(Mohandas Gandhi)

BE MY VALENTINE

Declan Gowran

As long as Love endures, St. Valentine's Day will always be celebrated like those other great milestones of Life such as births and marriages, deaths and divorces. But unlike these other emotional events governed by formal procedure, St. Valentine's Day is marked as the triumph of Hope over reality, sense over sentimentality, affection over infatuation, and above all: pure Love over base desire.

The modern St. Valentine might be regarded as the patron of prurience and misguided sincerity taken seriously. Red becomes the King of Colours, in fact it is the only colour permitted on the day. Hearts are the only suit on show in the deck of playing cards. A hundred-thousand silly rhymes record flippant feelings on often smutty and garishly cushioned greeting cards. Mysterious messages are written in disguised hands and signed off with the classic cliché: 'Roses are red, violets are blue; sugar is sweet and so are you: Guess Who?'

We can blame the Duke of Orleans for the introduction of St. Valentine Doggerel. When he was locked up in the Tower of London after the Battle of Agincourt in 1415, awaiting ransom, and missing his beautiful wife, he regularly wrote her love po-ems- valentines –to proclaim his undying devotion while keeping her on-side. History doesn't record if the Duchess was impressed enough to raise her husband's ransom in double-quick time.

Making your own Valentine Cards is a very popular pursuit for younger children bitten by the bug of cottage craftsman-ship. The cards are made in all shapes and sizes, decorated with a myriad of floral designs that pop-up and pop-out, fit-ted into baskets, filled with crepe tissue hearts and ribbons, and topped off by a crown in the style of a leftover Christmas cracker.

For highly strung teenagers a card that is smutty or funny or downright unintelligible is demanded, adorned with Stream of Consciousness thoughts spelling ciphers as 'Cool' in code. The more daring sender may even hint at their identity, by text, and suggest a lover's tryst in their den.

Even supposedly grounded grown-ups become wrapped up in the whole kitsch charade. Some become aspiring Poet Laureates overnight by proclaiming their fidelity forever in the small ads section of newspapers and magazines. Up market columnists conspire in the set-up by touting tips to star crossed suitors short on ideas, and less financially challenged, suggesting a romantic trip to Paris, a proposal on top of the Empire State Building, dinner with oysters and champagne or that very ultimate declaration of eternal love; a swim in the blue lagoon on that Greek island where Venus was created from a seashell.

Just to prove that our Valentine excess is genuine: wholesale pairs of caged love-birds are set free from the pet shops. Soft and cuddly toys are usurped by the ubiquitous Teddy Bear donning a sash bearing the invitation: 'Be my Valentine'. Diets are discarded over the scoffing of designer chocolates. Blood red roses are air-freighted by the dozens to sate the appetites of besotted fathers, sons and lovers, regardless of the weight of the carbon footprint left in their slipstream. Passion Fruit, of late has exacerbated this particular problem. But would we really have it any other way?

We can reliably fete the Romans for all this razzamatazz connected with the day. On February 15th the Festival of Lupercalia was celebrated in Ancient Rome to honour Faunus, the God of Flocks and Fertility. Like an embryonic form of Blind Date, the names of girls were placed in an urn and these were picked out by the young men who would pin the girl's name on the sleeve of their tunics, hopefully to be affixed permanently by Cupid's arrow. This gave rise to the saying: 'Wearing you heart on your sleeve'. In this Rite of Spring it was meant that smitten couples would pair-off and mate for life just like the birds.

With the legalising of Christianity under Constantine the Great many of the pagan festivals were abandoned or adapted. In the reign of the Emperor Claudius the Goth, an edict was proclaimed forbidding his legionnaires to wed as he considered single men without commitments made for fearless fighters. In defiance of the Emperor, St. Valentine, a priest and physician secretly married his soldiers. The saint was eventually exposed, imprisoned and beheaded and buried on the Flaminian Way in Rome on 14th February 269 AD. A basilica was subsequently erected on the site in 350 AD. On the very same day another St. Valentine was martyred at Terni, some 60 miles from Rome. This saint had been imprisoned for the seditious denouncing of Jupiter and Mercury as: 'Shameless, contemptible characters'. He had befriended his jailer's blind daughter, cured her and converted them to Christianity. It is now believed that both are the same St. Valentine imprisoned in Terni and martyred in Rome. February 14th was an auspicious date for the feast day as the Roman's celebrated the Festival of Juno, Goddess of Women and Marriage, and the wife of Jupiter on the same day.

St. Valentine's Relics have found a permanent home in the Church of Our Lady of Mount Carmel in Whitefriar Street in Dublin. Donated by Pope Gregory XVI to the Carmelite Fr. Spratt in 1835, the remains arrived in a steel casket on 10th November 1836 to be entombed with much ceremony. It is now a special place of pilgrimage for all those who seek their true love.

Swervo's return

Michael Henry

The ship's fog horn was not long rousing our man from his slumbers. He stretched and yawned and wished he had had a few hours more and in a proper bed at that. He admitted to himself that he had often slept in worse conditions; indeed in a great deal worse, but then he said to himself this was enough of the bad talk; for this weekend was to see a new beginning; things were going to change and for the better at that. The big clock over the shuttered bar told him that they would soon be docking.

As he watched most of the other passengers bustling away getting luggage and children and documents together, pressing up against the exit doors, ready to burst out when they were to be opened, he couldn't help thinking of greyhounds in traps waiting for the hare. Indeed he said it to a few but they didn't seem to appreciate his humorous observations. But his wry smile continued to attempt to burst past his three or four day stubble. He did not share the others concerns for he was travelling light - very light. Over the years, on occasion he would engineer a conversation around to that very point - travelling light.

"This way I can't lose or forget anything or have to worry about my things being stolen from me," he would tell those who would bother to listen, but there seemed to be less and less of those anymore. Fewer people seemed to bother about him as the years slipped by; they were too busy in their own little world. "They do not realise who I am" he sometimes muttered in frustration.

An elderly voice caught him off guard. "Are you not getting your belongings ready?" an old man enquired of him.

"Belongings, what belongings?" he snarled back and then he added "Sorry, I didn't mean to say it like that," but the man had already turned his head and leaned away. "That's what ye all do anymore....I don't bite." He was the last one off when the doors did finally open, with his only words uttered, "What time do the bars open?"

But it wasn't always like that. As he mulled over a mug of tea, he got a tap on the shoulder. "Swervo you old devil you, welcome back" It was Toucher Grimes and he was heading in the opposite direction waiting on the next sailing.

"It was only last week that a group of us were talking about you, Swervo and the great three in a row run? The likes of your display in those days hasn't been seen since you left". Swervo was holding a smile for longer than he had done in years. "They've won nothing, truly nothing since you left."

From pressing all the right buttons, Toucher veered over to touching a few wrong ones. "What made you leave so suddenly back then -- why no contact with anyone on our side since then -- what brings you back now-- what's with the limp?" He really capped it all with the line, "Any chance of a score for just a few weeks as the funeral might go on for a few days?" In the old days, Swervo would simply have assaulted him and it was his stock and trade solution to so many problems but he was supposed to be turning over a new leaf and so opted for a less dramatic course of reply, saying his train was due in a few minutes and he regretted he had to dash.

The walk down Main Street from the train station was uneventful till Sniffer Whelan dodged out of a cafe in front of him. "Ah, if it isn't the bold Swervo himself in the flesh, I do declare."

"Good evening Sniffer."

"And a lovely evening it is surely too bright enough, I grant you that, but they don't call me Sniffer for nothing and I'd nearly wager that you didn't travel all those miles, after all those years, just to wish your old centre forward buddy a good evening."

Swervo, since he had only the price of a few drinks, was prepared to take a little more ribbing but how much more he wasn't quite sure. "Ah, let me think now--perhaps, just perhaps, you have been made aware that Mrs. Jane O'Donnell has recently and tragically become the widow O'Donnell." Swervo could feel his face redden and his fists clench.

"As I recall ye were very great before John Joe stuck his beak in and of course when all papers were signed what could an honest God-fearing gentlemen do since dueling is no longer legal." Luckily for all concerned, a group had come out of the cinema, some of whom spotted Swervo and after shaking his hand and slapping his back, this time told him what he wanted to hear.

"Back where you belong" was one of most pleasing comments he heard. "Come in to Sean's for I'll have to stand you a drink or maybe two" was even better.

But there was a few in the company that expressed surprise at how Swervo and Sniffer appeared to be on good terms. After all, hadn't Swervo broken the window of Sniffer's bargain shop all those years ago and hadn't the guards found the goods at his place afterwards and only for Sniffer doing a deal for him to high-tail it, charges would have been pressed and he was looking at doing a long stretch, since he had been bound to the peace for assault many times.

How long would this pally stuff last they wondered, especially since it was said that Swervo knew all along that Sniffer had gone out of his way to introduce John Joe to Jane?

About two in the morning, Sniffer awoke to the sound of crashing glass. As quickly as he jumped out of bed to peer out the window, he saw the guards' car outside on the road and two guards leading a staggering man out from underneath the window's sill out of his shop to the sound of crunching glass. This man had a limp and yes, stubble - yes, it was him, surely. But how were they on the scene so quickly--did the cinema group standing across the road dare him to do it--did the guards know he was in town and likely to revisit the past - only in town a few hours? Or were they watching Sniffer himself?. By now his wife had joined him at the window.

"Isn't that the bloke that they were all talking about, being handcuffed? Why did those across not stop him. Why did he pick on our shop?" But Sniffer was stuck in every sense of the word. "Are they going to drive off with him, without first speaking to us? Here the window' now open. For God's sake man, do something-- say something?" But the best response Sniffer could muster out the open window was "Back where you belong surely."

Freedom to win

Tom Ramone

'Frankie! You coming?' asked Nicholas as they headed for the No. 18 bus. 'Be with you in a minute Nick. Just throwing a few DVD's in my bag', said Frankie as he rummaged through his crowded locker. He put Rocky 1 and 2, plus Raging Bull into his big worn Umbro sports bag. Other youngsters were filing in and out of Al's Boxing Club. It was 6.15 PM and Frankie would have to run if he and Nick wanted to catch the bus which was due at 6.18 PM. 'What are you like? You're always rooting for those boxing films when we're trying to catch a bus. We've missed a lot of buses because of you', Nick said as he and Frankie raced down the road towards the bus stop. Nick rummaged in his pockets for money for the bus fare. Like always he'd pay for Frankie. Not just because Frankie was his best friend but because Frankie was a superior boxer who taught Nick how to really fight. They both watched boxing DVDs of all the great movies and the real fights of Muhammad Ali. Frankie would have to watch the films at Nick's parents' house because his family didn't have a video or DVD player. Anyway Frankie's parents would not have approved of their only son watching such violence. There was enough of that mayhem all around them in the deprived area at which they lived. Drug abuse was rampant and local gang lords controlled the innocent young people who had little or no facilities. If Frankie's family could live somewhere else they would, but the cost of housing did not allow this possibility. Maybe one day their son, if educated properly, would help them to aspire to live in a better location.

"Wow! That was some punch Stallone gave to the other fella", Frankie said as he and Nick watched Rocky 1 for the umpteenth time. The Italian stallion was raining punches on his tough opponent. A lot of blood was being spilled. But it was a fight that was pure magic for the two boys. For them Rocky was the epitome of a real fighter; from a poor area and with all the odds stacked against him. Yet Rocky keeps training and fighting – he wants to win at all costs. Something inside the boys answers the call of this magic that is boxing. "One day I'm goin' to fight just like Rocky. I'm goin' to win and be heavy weight champion of the world", Frankie said, as Nick froze the screen showing Rocky bloodied and battered lifting the WBO Heavy Weight Champion of the world title belt. "That's a long way off. You're only fourteen. You got a lot of fightin' to do before you ever get to be a contender for the World Boxing Organisation. And how do you know you'll be able to fight at heavy weight level?" Nick said in a challenging tone of voice.

"It's my dream and I'm sticking with it. I have to believe in it. It's my only way out of this place. I don't want to wind up like my folks livin' out their lives surrounded by gurrier drug dealers and punishment shootings. I want a better life Nick and I'm gonna get there no matter what", Frankie said staring straight at his friend. Nick saw in Frankie's eyes a determination that he only saw once before – in the eyes of Muhammad Ali, the greatest boxer who ever lived.

Nick had all the posters of the great fighters from Rocky Marciano to Sugar Ray Leonard to Muhammad Ali and to the current greats of the heavy-weight boxing world. He also had all the DVD's and videos of the great fights. The one thing he saw in all those faces was the will to go beyond the pain, the blood, the closed swollen eye and the broken ribs to another level of being; a level which made winners stand out from the losers. A winner is someone who goes the extra mile that a loser won't those were the words that Nick remembered from the film Million Dollar Baby, if a woman could keep trying against the odds then why couldn't a boy keep trying? "I want to go with you Frankie", Nick said as he poured them both two glasses of lemonade.

"I don't want to finish up working at some job that I hate for the rest of my life. I want a better life Frankie", said Nick as he stared into his friend's eyes.

"Boxing is our passport out of here. Frankie do you know that Rocky Marciano holds the distinction of being the only

Heavyweight Champion of the World to retire undefeated. Like Rocky and Ali we can do it. I know we can! We will rock you and together we're goin' to rock the boxing world!" said Frankie in a loud booming voice that echoed through the thin walls of the house. A next door neighbour pounded on the bedroom wall and shouted, "Hey! Will you lot ever shut up in there; I'm tryin' to sleep"

But the two boys paid no heed to the next door neighbour and pounded down the stairs to put on another boxing film; this time Ali, the story of Muhammad Ali and his life of boxing which resulted in the freedom to win not just for Black America but for people with a goal and a vision no matter where they lived. As Nick and Frankie watched Ali dodge punches and jump around the ring they knew that one day they too would have the freedom to win.

RONNIE

Angela Macari

Being the daughter of a successful band leader and multi musician, has its advantages along with its disadvantages. For one thing, I spent my childhood surrounded by odd shaped cases containing various musical instruments, music stands, orchestrations, tapes and records, both vinyl and seventy eights that were heavy to hold and crackled loudly while being played on my Dad's beloved record player.

Emilio Macari, my late father could play Piano- Accordion, keyboards, Sax, Clarinet, drums; the list is endless!

He also gave music lessons which could be quite tedious for us in such a tiny house, where we'd have to regularly endure squeaks or bum notes from the efforts of students over and over. On top of which the hours that a musician's life involved, meant that we seldom saw him in the evenings or early mornings. Even in the afternoon, during his short break between gigs, he would go for a stroll around Dublin, or take in a matinee in the Savoy or Carlton Cinemas. This was the irregular and unpredictable life of a Band leader and his family!

However, there was an upside to the hectic and demanding lifestyle he chose, which was that we had regular visits from very high profile figures in the business, who'd invariably call for the loan of a musical arrangement, a record or simply to discuss a forthcoming gig. Well-known celebrities were an everyday occurrence for us kids. There was always a few of my Ma's scones, ham sandwiches or a Gateaux Swiss Roll kept handy for such events.

My first memory of the late Ronnie Drew was on one of these occasions, when he called in unexpectedly for a chat. I was sitting on our hall table with my friend playing with dolls, when the knocker on the big hall door of our house rapped loudly. I jumped down, running to open it. Outside was a cheerful man with a beard and a grin, who simply said in a deep voice 'Is Emilio there?'

My Dad came out and they went inside, talked and played records. When he was leaving, Ronnie pinched both my cheeks, laughed and said 'Ah me oul' Sagotia!' affectionately.

Over the years I realised through T.V., the radio and parents of friends how famous this gentleman, who to us was just Da's friend actually was!

Life is so funny! I joined Dublin Bus in 1982 and conducted the number 48A route for three years. My driver, a German called Bernt was a well known figure in the job, but he also had once been the Coach driver who took 'The Dubliners' on tour around Europe. What a coincidence!

I told him about my Dad's long standing friendship with Ronnie and how we had had lots of visits from the bowld Mr.Drew when I was but a young lass!

My mother Maureen often told us of the many plays that my Dad took her to, when Ronnie was an actor, which was before his Dubliner days. One such play was 'Richard's Cork Leg' and her anecdote about her reaction to the *flowery* language in it i.e. threatening to walk out, always makes me laugh!

Anyway, Bernt and I often swapped tales since he had many enjoyable drinking escapades, funny events and singing sessions to tell of. He also told me about the many beautiful places they toured in the good old days!

I became a bus driver in 1988 and Bernt and I parted company. But we kept in touch and some years later, he asked me if I'd like to go as his guest, to Ronnie Drew's house for Christmas Dinner. I was honoured and although it meant driving over snow covered Wicklow hills to get there, I will always remember the event as one of the nicest days of my life!

The Drew house was surprisingly similar to the house I grew up in, which sadly met a tragic fiery fate! It had a big hall door and an airy hallway just like the one where I first met Ronnie. Inside, there were many people along with Deirdre his wife, his children and grandchild. At the table, I was given a choice of a traditional Christmas Dinner, or Salmon En croute. In the end I had a taste of both. Deirdre was a tremendously talented cook.

After the meal everyone gathered around a table in the sitting room where Ronnie took out his acoustic guitar. We sang and some who didn't have to drive had a few drinks. I sipped a Coca Cola and just languished in the great man's company as he sang lots of old favourite Dubliner numbers. I even got a chance to perform my humble rendition of Simon and Garfunkel's 'The Boxer' on the beautiful guitar. Bernt was miffed at how I had so much to discuss with Ronnie about my late father, my mother and my brother Eugene, whom he admired as one of the finest guitarist in the land.

Bernt, who never went far without a camera took photographs. I put one on the wall in my little house in Saggart, where I lived until I got married in 2003 and moved to Rathcoole. Somewhere among my photo albums it hides and occasionally pops out and I admire the lovely guitar in my hand, Ronnie Drew sitting beside me and the both of us singing away. I have another of him lifting his grandchild high in that way that granddads do.

On leaving the party that night, Ronnie asked if there were any recordings of my Dad that he could have. We only had a cassette at the time, with my Dad performing a few of his favourites on piano. My Mother wouldn't part with it, but later on for her 80th birthday, my brother had it made into a C.D. There are only a few copies of which I have none alas!

The shock and disbelief I experienced last August on hearing of his passing, was overwhelming. Only a short time beforehand his beloved wife Deirdre had gone. Ronnie was ill for a while and he fought bravely. He appeared on a special tribute R.T.E. Late Late Show with lots of celebrities speaking of their claims to his friendship and inspiration. Proudly I told my husband of the happy memories I'm fortunate to have had, of this entertaining and unique man.

My mother and I were on a pilgrimage in Lourdes France when the news came, of the death of our good friend. We shed tears and lit him a candle at the Grotto. I hope one day to see my dad Emilio and Ronnie gigging in that great big theatre in the sky!

R.I.P. me oul' Sagotia!

BROWES PUCKAN

Mattie Lennon

Jim Browe above in Lacken
Had a virile puckan goat.
On his prowess, 'mid the bracken
There was every right to gloat.
The she-goats of the nation
He'd see they'd have a ball;
For a small remuneration
From their owners one and all.

Like wildfire round the mountain
His reputation spread,
And nanny-goats past countin'
With binder-twine were led.
The puck could fairly rise 'er
(He serviced great and small)
Like a P.R.O. for Pfizer
He pranced around his stall.

His prowess was discussed with pash,
Among the Wicklow hills.
In places like Donard and Clash
(Well known for thrills and spills)
When the media came to tape him
He was at their beck an' call.
And youths aspired to ape him
In every Parish Hall.

Some neighbour (no doubt jealous)
Told an agent of the State,
Who with pen and clipboard, zealous,
Arrived at Jim's front gate.
"An illicit stud's reported,
I must check out the call".
"I'm guilty" Jim retorted
"My back's against the wall".

The puck went through exacting tests
With techniques old and new,
And passed them all (despite their jests)
And with flying colours too.
He was registered in Dublin
As a stud could now walk tall:
With his new found status troublin'
The ones who hoped he'd fall

Now trading with impunity
Jim Browe could plainly see
A golden opportunity
To double up the fee.
The goat-house he had slated,
With fluorescent light an' all
And the price (in Euros) stated
On an ornamental spall.

Soon came an old reliable
With goat, and readies too.
The new regime seemed viable
But wait 'till I tell you;
The Puck decided he'd relax
And languished in his stall
While a licence stamped with sealing-wax
Hung framed upon the wall.

As more clients at the junction
Queued now with some chagrin
Erectile (goat) dysfunction
Appeared to have set in.
They coaxed him by being placid,
Then began to roar and bawl,
But the puck remained quite flaccid;
He wouldn't rise at all.

Said Jim "My little earner
Has turned out a farce"
As growing ever sterner
He aimed a kick in t' arse.
The puck glanced sideways, nervous,
At the parchment on the wall.
"Now I'm in the Civil Service
I'm supposed to do fuck-all".

THE COUNTY FINAL

John Cassidy

Pat Kennedy felt bad. He lit another Cigarette and swore he'd cut them down to twenty a day. A hacking cough racked his well-built frame as the acrid smoke cut into his throat. He threw back the bed covers and thought about getting up.

His bloodshot eyes focussed on the coloured print which dominated the wall at the end of the bed- the smiling face, black hair and the sweat soaked green and gold jersey, the Sam Maguire Cup held high above his head in gripping fists, and the autograph, "To Pat from Anthony, Croke Park 1992."

His idols, Molloy, McMullin, McHugh's, Reid, Walsh, the Boyles, Rambo, Walsh and all the rest of that history making squad, heroes all. His own short glory- days on the county. No diet then, no hangovers. A few weeks training, a few practice sessions, a few games and he was match fit.

He thought about last night. The selection meeting. The Captain's proposal that the team remained unchanged for the final. The sole dissenting voice- young Liam should be picked. As Chairman he could have vetoed it, but it seemed more diplomatic to hold his whist, it worked, they plumped for his experience rather than the fitness of the younger man. Afterwards, the Session in the bar. Half the team in the corner with the diet coke and glasses of orange. Big Jim helping out behind the counter.

The announcement of the team brought a buzz of excitement and kindled the fire of discussion. From every corner could be heard "if we get the first score...if midfield can....if big Jim" ...The talk flowed on, the fever of pre-final night grew. The pint tumblers mounted before him. It was on the way home that the doubts began. What did they really think of him?

Would he have held his place had he not been Chairman? The last few matches were agony; he was not fit and had played badly. After twelve years at mid-field and two at half back he dropped back to full back and was now in the corner.

There was good talent available from last year's minors. If he had hung up his boots last year young Sean would now be an automatic choice. He looked distastefully around the untidy room and rolled out of bed.

The match started quickly for him. The concentration and physical effort raised his spirits. The roar of the crowd got his adrenalin flowing. He wondered how they had managed before adrenalin was thought of. They had started well and knocked over a few points. He had played competently and his lack of pace had not been exposed. His opponent was young and very inexperienced. Initially the boy had stayed wide of the square waiting on the loose ball. A few digs in the ribs had soon sorted him out and he stayed well outfield after that.

By half time he felt better, he got his second wind and they were leading by four points. He had only been beaten once. The youngster had picked up a loose ball about forty yards out and had slipped by him on the outside. As he cut back diagonally towards goal, the boy shot hurriedly and the ball curled wide.

He began to feel his age in the second half. The opposition began to feed their left corner. The boy knocked over a great point from fifty yards out. On three occasions he had to bring down the youngster. He got away with it once, but points had been taken from the two frees. He thought about going off. So far they had only used one sub, sound lungs and fresh legs would keep the corner forward in check. Still they were a point in front and his experience would see him through.

The ball came high from midfield, he broke it down but it ran away towards the corner flag. The youngster went after it and lobbed it into the square; the full forward thundered in, a mass of bodies finished in the back of the net. A green flag went up, the left corner back stayed down. A sub came on, he could hardly go off now; he had better give it a few minutes until the team settled down. They got a point back but conceded another. Then Gallagher went off and the final replacement came on, it was now too late to lie down. The ball came down in his corner, he reacted too slowly, the youngster shimmied to his left and punched the ball over the bar before he got in his tackle.

Silently he listened to the referee's warning, a goal down and only minutes left. His opponent moved out following the kick out, he followed him grimly. The ball went up to the opponents square; the goal keeper grabbed it and drove it up the field. His opponent hesitated as it swung in the breeze. Pat slid past him went high in the air the ball went through his hands and cannoned of his chest. His impetus took him on to it, as it came off the ground it landed in his clutching hands. His run had taken him over the half way line, he steadied himself and drove it high for the posts, it fell short Big Jim rose and flicked it home. It was level scores.

The referee looked at his watch. The ball was driven out. A free in. Big Jim slotted it over the bar. The match was over. Pat Kennedy felt good. He thought there was at least another season in him.

Uncle Arthur's brew

Declan Gowran

The stand-off was becoming more physical and the abuse uglier. After the first provocative exchanges, the shoving and jostling then started as the burly Dublin Corporation navvies tried to enforce the City Sheriff's Order. Against this pressure the line of brewery workers tried to hold firm, their arms interlocked in the form of a chain, better to absorb the thrust of their protagonists. The brewery men groaned from the strain of holding their line:

"Quick! Run and summon the Master." The charge-hand shouted desperately to a terrified apprentice shoring-up the end of the line: "Run! Run! Before we break!"

On hearing the choked report of this surprise action of the Authorities from the gasping apprentice, the Master charged out of his office, across the yard, straight through the throng, and stormed into the eye of the fracas.

"Leave hold! Leave off!" He was yelling in fury. His head was pulsating, his face turning red with rage as he tried to stop the confrontation; and still the issue was contested.

The Master grabbed a discarded pick-axe, and brandishing it above his head, he swung the improvised weapon in great radial arcs, scattering the belligerents in his wake regardless of their allegiance.

"Desist at once!" he bellowed with menace directed at the city council's navvies: "Desist now! This is my water, my river water God given and free. I have swam in it, fished it, and will drown in it if necessary to preserve my right to draw from it. I shall never relinquish that right, neither to you or your superiors. Go tell them that! Arthur Guinness fulfils his promises and orders it so. Now Go!"

The navvies slinked back in retreat chastened by the defiance of the man who had challenged them across the disputed watercourse of the River Liffey like a colossus. The City Sheriff, who was nominally in charge of the enforcement of the right of the City Council to reclaim the watercourse, said afterwards in a statement of 'saving face' that the city's right to the watercourse had been asserted; but it would have been wrong to proceed under the circumstances.

In order to forestall any such further action by Dublin Corporation Arthur Guinness filed a Bill against it with Injunctions for the ground, pipes and Liffey Watercourse supplying the St. James's Gate Brewery. In 1779 Dublin Corporation did indeed instigate a further foray to recover the watercourse only to discover to their consternation that a wall had been erected to enclose it and protect it from just such incursions.

The watercourse dispute dragged on, until in May 1785 in order: 'To put an end to suit', Dublin Corporation invited Arthur Guinness to become 'A tenant to ground for watercourse and the pipes at Echlin's Lane of 2 inch bore thereto under lease with Rainsford at £10 per annum rent.' Arthur agreed and with both sides' honour intact the watercourse dispute was finally resolved.

The Watercourse Dispute is one of the few recorded incidents in the life of Arthur Guinness the founder of the famous St. James's Gate Brewery in Dublin. Arthur was born in Celbridge, County Kildare in 1725 to Richard Guinness and his wife Elizabeth, who was a daughter of the prosperous Reid family of North Kildare. Richard had worked as a groomsman for the family before falling in love with Elizabeth. Constrained by their respective positions and the social inhibitions of the time, they decided to elope and marry. Richard subsequently found employment as an agent and rent collector for Dr. Arthur Price, the Anglican Archbishop of Cashel who had his seat and estate in Celbridge.

Arthur had three brothers: Richard who was to follow him into the brewery trade, Benjamin who was to become a merchant in Dublin and Samuel, known as the Goldbeater. He also had two sisters: Frances, who was to marry into the Darley family of developers in Dublin, and Elizabeth who was to marry Benjamin Clare who was related to Richard's second wife, Elizabeth Clare who owned the White Hart Inn in Leixlip, County Kildare.

There is some dispute as to the origins of the family. One theory suggests that Richard of Celbridge was the grandson of an adventurer called Gennys from the town of the same name in Cornwall who accompanied Cromwell to Ireland in 1649 as a foot-soldier and remained after the Cromwellian Settlement to carve out a living. Far more acceptable to Arthur Guinness and his family was the claim that he was descended from the noble Magennis Clan of County Down. The use of the Magennis Coats of Arms during his own lifetime would have lent an exalted status to a mere merchant family and established an ancient Anglo-Irish pedigree which would have suited the politics and social class requirements of the day.

Richard of Celbridge proved to be a diligent and honest employee and was apparently well liked by Dr. Price and his tenants. Arthur also acted as an agent for Dr. Price, and the first recorded example of the signature that was to become famous on every label of Guinness was the signing of a lease for meadowland near Oldtown, County Kildare in 1756.

In accordance with the culinary practices of the time it would have been accepted that the larger households would have a small brewery attached to provide beer and ales for the kitchen and table as these refreshments were more potable than the drinking water generally then available which would have often been contaminated particularly in larger towns and cities. It would appear that Richard had become interested in brewing as a hobby and had become quite proficient in producing a passable brand of homemade beer. The basic ingredients of beer and ale were roasted barley which was malted or soaked with water to provide wort which was then dried and flaked; hops to give it the bittersweet flavour and yeast to ferment it with alcohol. The mature liquid was then strained into kegs. Leftovers like barm went to the baker, and spent hops used as animal feed.

Richard involved Arthur in the brewing process at the bishopric and soon developed a talent for the art. But whereas Richard was content to confine himself to home-brewing; Arthur saw through the froth of his first brewing efforts to detect a business opportunity and a lifetime career in the making. It must have been during this initial trial brewing period that he formulated his successful business model based on the finest of raw materials like Kildare Barley and English Hops, the correct quantity of ingredients especially of yeast, the time-weighted brewing of the mixture, and the most stringent quality control such as the purity of the water to fix the taste of the product.

Richard's first wife died in 1742 and he subsequently courted and married Elizabeth Clare, a widow and proprietor of the White Hart Inn in Leixlip. Attached to the inn was a small brew-house and it was here that young Arthur set-up shop as an independent brewer, translating his own brewing theories into practice, as it were, on a slightly larger scale than Dr. Price's kitchen brewery; and developing his own vision for the future.

Dr. Arthur Price died in 1752 and left £100 in his Will to both Richard and Arthur. With this money to back him, Arthur persuaded his father to purchase the lease of a small brewery beside the iron and linen mills along the river Liffey at Leixlip. It was a bona fide brewery ready equipped with the minimum of refurbishment costs and an endless water supply from the Liffey. Arthur moved in on September 25th 1756. His younger brother Richard was taken on as an apprentice while Arthur would be the Master Brewer. As manager of a brewery Arthur would now have to research and source raw materials, oversee the brewages and the marketing and sales of the products, the efficient running of the plant, and transportation. North Kildare was more populated then than in more recent times and large towns such as Maynooth and Lucan were readily accessible; but Arthur's life plan was to be still more ambitious.

Arthur joined the Corporation of Dublin Brewers in April of 1759: the recognised Guild of St. Andrew's for his trade in order to establish his credentials in a city that was largely governed through its 25 trade guilds represented on the city council. Thanks to his forthright character and no nonsense approach and negotiating skills, Arthur became a Warden of the Corporation of Dublin Brewers in 1763, and then Governor in 1767.

Arthur had resolved to acquire a suitable brewery in Dublin, then a city with Capital status boasting its own Parliament housed in the pillared Parliament House opposite Trinity College designed by Sir Edward Lovett Pearce in 1729. The great Georgian developments of Luke Gardiner and his son Lord Mountjoy, and of the Fitzwilliam and Merrion Estates were transforming the fetid medieval old town into a metropolis of wide streets and elegant squares of parkland and red-bricked townhouses. The great mansions of the nobility followed led by the earl of Kildare who constructed his home on Molesworth Fields; and the exceptional Public Buildings like the Royal Exchange on Cork Hill designed by Thomas Cooley in 1769. These edifices opened up new vistas of splendour to enthral the ever growing milieu of gentry gazing across the changing Dublin skyline. These would be Arthur's market as each household always had a barrel of beer on tap in the cellar: and the bigger the household, the bigger the barrel it required. Arthur would also have to consider supplying inns and hostelries and taverns against the competition of another one hundred odd breweries. These breweries would offer *doucers* or inducements like introductory gifts to prospective customers, free barrels, credit allowances and 'pay-up by' rebates. In addition the majority of taverns were known euphemistically as 'Open Houses' under the sole control of certain breweries.

Arthur had a number of advantages going for him and these were his expertise in the trade, the quality of his product, his single-minded business energy, his contacts and a determined streak of ruthlessness in obtaining his objectives. One of his earliest coups was to be appointed Official Brewer to the Viceroy and grandees in Dublin Castle in 1779 which effectively was giving his product the Royal Seal of approval, and which inevitably lead to his Knighthood for charitable works coupled with his services to the Crown.

On his excursions into Dublin seeking suitable new premises for the expansion of the business, Arthur identified an old disused brewery at the junction of Thomas Street and James's Street in the Liberties of Dublin that was available for immediate lease from the Rainsford family. On an acre of neglected ground stood a spacious dwelling with outhouses and stables for twelve horses, a fish pond, a mill, two malt-houses and a copper brewing vessel that was stained green from a surfeit of damp years of idleness. Despite its decay, Arthur saw its potential and was motivated to make an offer for the brewery. Using a shrewd stratagem Arthur negotiated the lease of St. James's Gate at a rental of £45 per annum for a period of 9,000 years, signed the lease on September 24th 1759 and moved in on December 31st 1759.

Arthur concentrated on the brewing of ales and beer in the early years. It was only from April, 1799 that the brewery was to concentrate on brewing its brand of Plain Porter, and the stronger, world famous: 'Extra Stout Porter'. The term porter was taken from the porters of the London markets who had taken to relish this highly hopped dark brown beer that was stronger than table beer, but weaker than traditional ale. Porter had been brewed by Harewood in Shoreditch in the East End of London in 1722 and first sold and served in the 'Blue Last' pub in Shoreditch. It was said that the drink was accidentally brewed because Harewood had burnt the roasting barley and had sold the resultant dark liquid cheaply to the porters of the London markets. The thirsty porters couldn't get enough of it, ensuring its success and popularity. In the fullness of time this accident became attributed to Richard and Arthur, while other connoisseurs insisted that certain vermin were added to the fermentation process to give 'Uncle Arthur's Brew' more 'body'; while still others insisted that Arthur's secret recipe for Extra Stout Porter had been stolen from an enclosed Order of Monks who had produced the stronger beer to improve the muscular productivity of the workers labouring in their dairy and farm and scriptorium!. The 'Harp' trademark was adopted in the 1860's.

The London porter was brewed with soft water, not hard and grew in flavour with keeping in the cask. Porter kept longer than beers or ales so that the stock could be stored longer and provide for a longer shelf life for sale with less wastage from staleness. Although porter was originally called 'stale' it became 'stout' as it improved with age. With the introduction of Patent Brown Malt Arthur brewed his 'Triple X Stout' recipe. Patent Brown Malt was a more highly coloured malt that gave the porter a more caramelized consistency and produced a saving on extract because it required smaller portions for the recipe. The stronger the porter the dearer it was and Guinness Extra Stout sold at (4d) 4 pence a quart which was dear enough considering the average industrial wages of the day varied between 5 and 10 shillings. St. James's Gate competed with London imports such as 'Pharoah', 'Huff-Cup' and 'Knockdown' which latter brand name might hint at the knock-out potency of the brew if taken to excess.

In time porter became a tonic given to expectant mothers to build up the iron in the blood. It was also offered to blood donors to revive their energy in those misguided and naive days before the introduction of more severe drinking laws. Stout of course is used to fortify foods such as puddings, cakes and the ubiquitous stews and pies.

The 'Pint of Plain' became an immortal cultural icon with the introduction of The Working Man's Friend by Flann O'Brien:

'When things go wrong and will not come right though you do the best you can

When life is dark as the hour of night: a Pint of Plain is your only man!'

Mention must be made of the 'Large Bottle': the Guinness of choice for the hard working and hard drinking Irish Navvy, docker, and farm labourer. Thus the famous ritual was instituted of the double pour of the porter at 45 degrees angle into the glass, causing the gush of the bubbling brown brew with the frothy settling time of three minutes as the creamy head was held aloft by the action of the brewing gases before the pint was passed through the lips.

When Arthur first began brewing at St. James's Gate the excise duties on beers and ales was a perennial bugbear for the Corporation of Dublin Brewers. As well as high local tariffs on beers brewed for the home market there were higher export taxes of beers exported to England in contrast to a lower rate of taxes on beers exported from England into Ireland. These excise anomalies had become so skewed that at one time Arthur had threatened to close St. James's Gate and set up a new operation in North Wales; and he had even gone so far as to travel there to reconnoitre suitable sites, but was unable to find one. In his position as Governor of the Corporation of Brewers he petitioned Parliament for a fairer deal for his profession; and as he was related by marriage to Henry Grattan, he was able to elicit his support to further the interests of brewers and industry in general.

In June, 1761 Arthur married Olivia Whitmore, the heiress and Ward of William Lunell of a well-to-do Dublin merchant family. She brought with her to the brewery lodge a dowry of £1,000 and the charitable outlook of a progressive woman of her times. Arthur himself had supported altruistic organisations since his earlier years as a Knot of the Servants of St. Patrick in Kildare. He supported the Dean and Chapter of St. Patrick's Cathedral and the pupils of St. Patrick's Choir and Grammar School of 1432 with a bounty. He also served as treasurer and governor of the Meath Hospital. He founded the first Sunday School in Ireland in 1786. Arthur and Olivia had ten surviving children and it was his namesake Arthur the Second who was to succeed his father on his death in January, 1803 at the age of 78. Arthur was buried near his mother in Oughterard Cemetery in County Kildare.

THE GOOD AULD DAYS

Mark Bolger

'Next stop!' the driver announced, 'Dublin. Please place your ticket chip against the seats in front of you.'

The doors dilated shut. John missed the good auld days of diesel fumes and traffic jams. He'd been griping against change in the company for one hundred and twenty years now. Even before his first rejuvenation, he realised with a grin.

Engaging gear, he rose from the French plasti-crete.

His latest bugbear with the company was they were trying to introduce a twenty-six hour week. He was safe behind the protection of his pre Twenty-Eighteen contract, but what about the new drivers coming in and being forced to work the medieval hours now demanded.

He was entitled to the quarterly re-juve treatments. Head therapy for his family was expected. What with the job making him come home cranky, adding the pressures life in the late twenty-second century forced on everyone. Qualifying for four continent free travels for him and his family was down to service time in.

Accelerating the bus past Mach three, John knew he might end up in the office for speeding, but he didn't care. Not now they were trying to restrict *his* travel entitlements.

Nodding at another driver whizzing past he noticed a passenger stood next to him; face like thunder, glaring through the field separating them.

'Bloody service,' the passenger snarled, thumping the barrier, 'good for nothing...'

Flicking a switch, a field, complete with sound damper, enveloped the irate traveller.

Smiling, John realised change was not all bad.

THAT IS WHERE WE ARE ALL HEADED

Scotty Sturgeon

How many of us take newspapers for granted? In this modern sophisticated age, with consumer protection etc, one is seldom fooled, but not so long ago, the statement that "all that is in print is true" was widely accepted. Take a full page advertisement from the Irish Independent of December 4th 1929 for example. The ad was for "Whites electric Comb" which was claimed to "restore dead hair roots." Only those whose head was like a billiard ball could not be helped. Although the user felt nothing the comb passed "millions of electric waves from hair root to hair root..." Waking them up and bringing them to life. Just like pouring life-giving water to parched soil.

Dandruff is stopped within three days. Straight hair takes on a natural wave. The hair already on your head becomes strong and full of light and colour. New hair grows from old dead roots. Bald patches are quickly covered. Greyness disappears as the new hair grows. In a few weeks the hair is only grey at the ends and full of colour right down each hair to the root. As it grows you "cut the greyness off."

The comb's electricity came from a little battery in the handle and the manufacturer supplied a little testing-bulb so that one could ascertain whether the current was "on or off." The ad asked pertly "Are you in the least bit doubtful?" stating that 120,000 satisfied customers were, until they sampled the product. The comb could be purchased for ten shillings, or one pound for the Deluxe gold plated model.

But who would be so silly to swallow such a ridiculous story. In 1929 very few Irish people knew anything at all about electricity; the rural electrification scheme for example caused much wonder and bewilderment when it came in 1946. The technology required to place a pencil-thin battery in a comb was hardly available then, so one has to assume the Whites of London were hoaxers.

Deceit of course is universal. When I was a lad the girls in our neighbourhood had a maxim which warned against deceit in prospective suitors, "Beware of men whose eyebrows meet, for in their hearts is found deceit." Another maxim however thankfully ruled out that one, it was, "Love is blind" and consequently many gentlemen with interlocking eyebrows found little difficulty in obtaining spouses.

Deceit has been advantageous to some and misfortune to others since the dawn of time. Even in the Bible, the first reference to a relationship or partnership, that of Adam and Eve,was disrupted by deceit. Deceit is the camouflage of poachers, the finesse of safe-crackers, the expertise of smugglers and the polished tool of every confidence trickster imaginable.

Perhaps deceit has never been recognised as such. Take for example a work of expressionistic art submitted to the Tate Gallery in London in 1972 by one Carl Andre. In 1965 Andre bought 120 bricks from a brickyard, arranged them in a low pile on the floor of the art gallery, and priced them at 12,000 dollars, he had no customers.

He was short of money so he returned the bricks to the brickyard and received a refund of what he had paid for them. In 1972 a director of the Tate Gallery saw a photo of the exhibit and offered the gallery the required amount for them. The Tate Trustees had approved the purchase in the normal manner. Delighted Andre returned to the brickyard only to find it closed, but he managed to find more bricks and in due course sent them to London with instructions for their assembly.

The sculpture was made up of 120 bricks since Andre stated "120 is the number richest in factors," and were catalogued in the Tate as "120 firebricks, purchased from the John Weber Gallery N.Y. 1972."

Some questions however remained unanswered, despite the furore the bricks caused in the media at the time. Could the sculpture be considered a fake since the bricks were not the ones originally exhibited? Was the whole affair a deliberate publicity stunt to draw crowds to the gallery? The crowds did come.

With regard to further deceit in art Van Dyck, the Flemish painter only actually painted seventy pictures; over 2,000 of his "Works" have been sold. Such is the expertise of the master forger that even highly acknowledged experts were duped. In 1935 five American millionaires paid an average 300,000 dollars apiece for the Mona Lisa, without it ever leaving the Louvre. Thirty of Van Gogh's paintings in European galleries have been found to be forgeries.

Deceit or not the master forger has always commanded a certain amount of respect among the common people. The Dutch painter Hans Van Meegeren is a good example of a forger come folk hero. His paintings were so good he fooled many leading art dealers and collectors including Hermann Goering. When arrested in 1947, as a Nazi collaborator on the grounds he had sold Goering the famous painting, Christ and the Adulteress, by Vermeer, he admitted it was a master fake. Chemical and x-ray examination proved his statement true and while in prison he painted another Vermeer, Jesus in the Temple to further prove his point.

Then there was Warren Madill who sold "Old Masters" for as little as one hundred pounds in London. Madill always claimed he never made a dishonest penny in his life, selling his fakes for what they were in his aptly named Fine Art Fake shop near Regents Park.

Finally, the American evangelist Arthur Blesset who toured the world lugging a life sized cross everywhere with him and getting locked up, stoned, and beaten for his trouble. He claimed while converting South American heathens he trained a local parrot to recite passages from the New Testament in Spanish. He planned to release the parrot in the jungle to teach the holy writ to all the other parrots.

"Imagine it," he said, "the whole jungle full of parrots singing God's praise."

His plans floundered when a low flying aircraft spraying mosquitoes infected his feathered friend, which eventually keeled over without passing on any of the good news.

This story is unequalled, surely, in the annals of parrot anecdote.

THE HOUSE

Thomas Carroll

I arrived at 2.20 PM in the afternoon at No. 22 Ailesbury Road. The autumn sun was illuminating the front windows of the two storey Georgian house. The estate agent had not yet arrived. I was here one hour ahead of schedule. I wanted to get a feel for the exterior first because it gives you a good idea of the condition of the interior. The previous owner was a writer and dealer in fine art. He certainly liked plants; the front garden was absolutely beautiful. A Japanese maple tree was beginning to change leaf colour from green to deep red. The red brick of the house looked warm in the October sunshine. I peered in through one of the front windows – all the furniture had been removed except for an old writer's bureau. I could hardly wait for the estate agent to arrive. I wanted desperately to explore this fine house.

Finally, at 3.35 PM the lady arrived. "Hi Mr. O'Hagen; dreadfully sorry to have kept you waiting," she said.

"Oh don't worry; I've been looking at the magnificent front garden. It truly is a superb residence," I said.

"I'm delighted to hear to you say that Mr. O'Hagen. Well we better go inside," she said turning the key and opening the front door. There was a nice smell of fresh ground coffee. Someone must have made it so that the aroma would filter throughout the house. I knew this old estate agent trick, having bought several houses over the years. The hall was very impressive, especially the fine stairs which was wide enough for three people to walk side by side. I looked up at the window at the top of the stairs – sunlight was streaming in and casting a nice light on the burgundy coloured walls.

I wanted to say that I'd buy the house there and then. But I thought it would be better to get a proper guided view so as to fully appreciate the place. The living room was quite big. I imagined that a large dining room table would look well in the middle of the room. It would be perfect for entertaining guests and my wife Anne would enjoy the freedom that space gives.

"As you can see Mr O'Hagen just off the dining room is the kitchen which is much larger than you would find in a new house. So if you like cooking, you will have ample space to create that dish of your dreams," she said with a smile.

"As a matter of fact I do like to cook and so does my wife Anne," I said.

"Shall we go upstairs and take a look at the bedrooms," she said. The view from the master bedroom was terrific. You could see the whole front garden and the sea which was no more than a quarter mile away. No problem in fitting a king-size bed in this lovely room. I knew immediately this was the house of my dreams. My wife Anne would be delighted with it! In the end I bought the house and everything has worked out perfectly.

WHEN ALL ROADS LED TO TARA

John Cassidy

How far back can the beginning of our road system be traced? Few travellers by road from Belfast or Galway realise that for part of the way at least, they are using the road along which Cuchulain drove his fiery chariot. When we think of ancient roads we think of the Famous "Rome Roads." In view of this it is interesting to note that the Romans borrowed most of their words for wheeled vehicles from the Celtic languages and their knowledge and use of these aids to transport were also borrowed. It is possible that even the accepted term "Roman Road" was a development of an original Celtic idea.

That ancient Irish were well supplied with roads we learn from our ancient literature and from the Brehon Laws where many rules for making and repairing roads were laid down. Those roads were not like our present hard smooth roads but neither were they mere tracks. They were constructed according to knowledge and needs of the period, sometimes laid with wood and stone, sometimes not, but always wide and level enough for chariot and horse traffic.

There were, in fact, seven different kinds of roads, which were classified according to their size and purpose. The largest or main roads were called Sliges. There were five of these and they all led from Tara in County Meath to the adjoining provinces. A Slige, we are told, was made for the passing of chariots by each other, for the meeting of two chariots of the largest size, a Kings chariot and a Bishop's chariot, so that each might go freely past the other.

The next in size was a Ramut, it was an open space or way that led to the forts of Kings and every owner whose land came up to it was bound to cleanse his own part of it. Next we come to the Bothar, the word in general use at the present day for a road. We read that 'two cows fit on it, one lengthwise ways and one athwart; their calves and their yearlings fit on it along with them i.e. each calf walking beside its mother for if the calves were behind them the cow that followed would gore the calf in front of her.

A Rot was a small road with no fence. It was made for the horses of a mansion and there was room on it for a one-horse chariot. A Set was smaller than a Rot, a path for one animal, wide enough for a single cow or horse.

Lastly we have the tuaghrota, and the imrota. The former was a farmer's road, such as he makes when he is permitted or buys a right of way from his farm to a nearby main road, or to a mountain for the convenience of sending cattle to graze on it, or for bringing home turf. The latter was a small by-road made for the convenience of communication, or to connect two main roads.

The five main roads which led from Tara are frequently mentioned in ancient manuscripts, and we can form a fairly accurate picture of their routes. The Slige Asail ran from Tara due west towards Lough Oriel in Westmeath and divided the Kingdom of Meath into two equal parts, north and south. The Slige Midhluachra extended northwards towards Slane, north of the Boyne and on through the Moyry Pass, north of Dundalk, and round the base of Slieve Fuaidh, near the present Newtown Hamilton in County Armagh to the Palace of Emain.

The Slige Mor [Great Highway] led south west from Tara, till it joined the Esker Riadha [a long natural wavy ridge, formed of gravel] running across almost the whole Country from Dublin to Galway and divided it in half somewhere near Clonard. Besides these five great Highways which are constantly referred to, in the Annals and other old documents notice numerous individual roads. In the Annals of the "Four Masters" there are 37 ancient roads mentioned with the general name Bealach , nearly all with the descriptive epithets, e.g. Bealagh Mugha, better known as Ballymoon near Carlow.

STARLIGHT

Ronnie Hickey

Stars
That appear
To last forever
Might look down
If they could
Might envy
If they could
The misting breath
Of a newborn lamb
Its fleeting dream
Of living.

A MATTER OF SPACE

Thomas Carroll

In Earth time they had been voyaging for 20 centuries through the vast cosmos. They came from a galaxy so distant that it is not observable even with the Hubble space telescope. They were now approaching earth and had made the long journey to help us in our efforts to achieve world peace. The year is 2020 and the world is teetering on the verge of outright nuclear holocaust. China has threatened to use nuclear weapons in its bid to take control of Japan and Korea. A ten megawatt nuclear device has already been detonated in the Sea of Japan causing serious pollution to the mainland. The USA has come to the aid of Japan by deploying a large air and sea presence. Seven Trident submarines, each with a nuclear attack capacity ten times that of the Hiroshima bomb, are situated 35 miles out to sea. Six aircraft carriers, each with a complement of three hundred fighter jets and powerful surface to air missiles are positioned 40 miles from Japan's coastline.

Now the alien craft was within 10 million miles of planet earth. The commander of the great ship checked to see if his invisibility shield was activated. A flashing orange light told him it was. "Proceed at half speed" he said in a deep voice. Earth's radar system would not detect the massive ship because the material it was constructed from would not show up on any human radar system. The commander viewed the blue planet on his screen and gave the command for the great ship to spread out [break up]. In an instant the giant space ship had become six smaller craft; each of which was invisible and could move at incredible speeds in any direction. The commander and his chosen aliens were in craft number one which was now cruising at two thousand feet over the Hudson River in New York. Of course no humans could see the ship; it was totally invisible and completely silent.

China's military bases and her cities could be annihilated in a matter of thirty minutes or less. Therefore the situation on earth looks very uncertain, peace hangs in the balance. It is known that the Chinese have long-range missiles armed with nuclear warheads aimed at prominent American and European cities. World war three is about to begin.

The space travellers who are now landing their large space craft in a remote region of the South Pole have been observing mankind for many centuries by the use of special invisible probes orbiting the earth. They have seen how the human race has developed into what it is today a greedy, war mongering species intent on destroying not only itself but the entire planet. The aliens have seen how little humans have learned from history. Now these other life-forms have come from deep space to prevent mankind from self-destruction. The extraterrestrials realise their mission must be successful because time is running out for human peace. They know that contact must be made with the leaders of both the USA and China. The creatures also realise that this revelation will come as both a shock and a surprise, the entire world will focus on the strange visitors.

The Aliens have evaded all radar and military tracking devices by using far superior technology they have remained invisible. They are able to silence the sound of their craft's powerful engines. For three days and nights the Aliens have monitored the situation in the north Pacific by sending out smaller spacecraft to obtain visuals of human activity on both land and sea. Again these smaller space ships have remained invisible so that a complete reconnaissance has been achieved. The tension is high and the extraterrestrials know that a full scale nuclear war could begin at any moment. They communicate through computers so that we can understand them – an altogether satisfactory process, since our own electronic equipment is capable of phenomenal processing speed. "We must act fast. Don't you think Commander Vollex?" a serious faced alien asked.

"Obviously it is our intergalactic duty to save the human race from destruction. They are still at a primitive stage in their development as a species. We have no other choice but to intervene." said Vollex. "If we make our presence known to the US government they will accept our offer of assistance."

The USA is the first government to be contacted because they have had more contact than any other government with life forms from outer space. The US are delighted that these extraterrestrials have become involved in the struggle to save planet earth. The Japanese are also relieved that these strange beings are going to be on their side. As far as the Japanese are concerned the gods have answered their prayers. However, the Chinese government are not impressed with the intervention of the extraterrestrials. The Chinese explain to the aliens that this matter is none of their business and that interfering with events here on earth is not on. The Chinese want to take over Japan and Korea, thereby creating a gigantic superpower in the Far East. The Chinese threaten the aliens with a nuclear attack unless they are allowed to go ahead with their plans. But this threat is futile because the alien spaceship is invisible and its location is still secret. Commander Vollex sat in his big command chair facing the big screen observing the beauty of planet Earth. Today it looked particularly blue and he could clearly make out the great area which China occupied. His webbed right hand slid open a red cover which concealed the ship's lethal weapon – a laser guided nuclear device which was three thousand times stronger than any nuclear war head on Earth. "We must consider carefully the implications of destroying China. It would appear their government are unwilling to co-operate in a peaceful settlement. What a shame we will have to destroy 1.2 billion people all because of 10 war mongers!" Vollex said in his mind communicator. The assembled crew nodded in sad agreement. The anger of the Chinese increases when they discover that none of their nuclear armed missiles will launch because their computer controlled attack and defence systems have been completely crippled by a laser signal sent from the alien ship.

The US and European forces offer china an ultimatum – a chance to negotiate a peace deal. "Look here you crowd of barbarians you can't just go around possessing other countries. The world just doesn't work that way!" roared Colonel Platt, his face a torrid red colour. He paused to wipe a band of sweat which had appeared across his forehead.

"Pardon me for saying so sir, but I doubt if the Chinese will react favourably to a slightly too heavy-handed approach. I mean we must consider the economic importance of China to the West", said Major Rice, who knew how angry Colonel Platt could become in any course of events.

"You know damn well that I am aware of their value to our western economies. I'm not just an army big wig you know!" Platt retorted, looking indignant as usual. He hated having obvious facts spelt out to him.

"Well why don't the Chinese watch a re-run of the TV series 'V' then they might very quickly come round to working with the aliens. My attitude is if you can't beat them – join them!" Platt said as a military transport plane flew low over his office rattling all the windows. Reluctantly the Chinese accept the offer and plans are put in place to secure the future of Japan and Korea. China will have to reduce its stockpile of nuclear weapons and sign a non-proliferation treaty. For the foreseeable future economic sanctions are imposed on China and trade with other countries will be severely curtailed. Also the island of Hong Kong will be allowed to become independent of China – the place will become designated as a tax avoidance / offshore account type place.

The Aliens have been successful in their mission to save mankind and for a month or so they remain on earth to survey the scenery especially around Florida, Hawaii and Ireland. The extraterrestrials have regular weekly meetings with the Chinese to make sure that they keep to the terms of the agreement. After travelling half way across the universe the aliens have no time for dirty tricks or superpowers reneging on peace deals. Everything seems to be in order and the Chinese government are determined to keep to the letter of the agreement. So the day came when the Aliens announced their departure from planet earth. All has worked out well and the weird looking creatures get ready for their long voyage home. It will take them close to two decades of earth time to reach their own planet, which in their time is about two hours and a bit. Yes, they are as happy as pigs in shit, they will have achieved their mission – peace on earth. And a job well done is always worth being happy about. Plus the aliens are taking with them thousands of plant and animal specimens so that they can replicate them back on planet Zenda. They are particularly interested in the health potential of our great jungles and forests. "Hopefully we will create another environment similar to Earth", says Vollex in an enthusiastic voice.

Commander Vollex gives the all-clear to apply full thrust to attain light speed. The pilot using his webbed hand slides the thruster-lever fully forward and in the twinkling of an eye the great space ship has vanished. There are a lot of broken hearts left behind on earth especially amongst young women who were beginning to take a liking to the long haired creatures from planet Yipchita. Even members of the gay community were in tears, especially in San Francisco, at the departure of the incredibly handsome aliens who had physical bodies that were the envy of many a queer man!

THE GREY HERON

Thos Maher

in the shallow water
there sweeps a cold wind
a lone heron hangs out
and boldly stalks
a fish, or an eel maybe
it feels that is there,
then with startling speed
it pricks its prey.
Death-so sudden
but winter has come.
Still, when all is done
and happy with its lot
this gaunt bird
arches its wings
and is silently away.

DONTCHA JUS LOVE
A GOOD DEADLINE !!!

Billy Fleming

How does one imagine the future will look back upon Èire 2009....a year auspicious for its position at the bottom of just about every graph that ever graphed the course of anything that could be graphed? House prices, car prices, petrol prices, gas (Yes we *are* still governed by the English rules of speech) prices and the price of almost every commodity whose value we remain ignorant of all came tumbling down after a prolonged period of imitating a Satun V on its way to God knows where. There was no limit to our onward and upward march to financial independence and then some more added on.

"Oh dear, Oh dear, Oh dear",a few naysayers managed to croak before being dismissed by the new gentrified Irish Citizenry or indeed being invited to commit suicide by one of our more colourful ex-Taoisigh as he headed off for a new career on the "Lecture Circuit."

Did we,"de peeeple" even consider the serious world-wide implications of Allowing an ex-Taoiseach venture abroad talking, what we now know to be high octane nonsense,to some of the World's Movers and Shakers who would actually pay $2,000 a plate to eat and listen to vivid descriptions of how to bottle coloured smoke and then market it at a substantial profit to folks who have loads of money combined with almost no knowledge of what to spend it on.

Maybe we did, but I suspect we preferred to bask in the reflected glory inherent in any foreigner wanting to pay to listen to anything spoken by a native northside Dub.

Gosh but it gave us all a sense of being suddenly important.... of having arrived !

And by Golly, didn't it just stick it to them old Imperialists who had tried, but failed to impose their dour Protestant work ethic upon us and just look at the mess they're in now!

And yet...and yet......most folks not yet at pension age can remember a past where money, possessions and associated other things were not traded freely or even possessed by the average workin` man...no sir they were not !

I can still remember My Father bringing home his first "new" car...a 1950 something Ford Popular then already over 10 years old and now expected to replace his bicycle. From that day forward my Father never owned a new car and was always reluctant to spend more than £100 on whatever replacement was deemed necessary for the old one.

There was never a chance of my Da buying a car because of its colour, or its badges...his first concern would be to see if it would take a tow-bar. Whatever car was operated was run pretty much into the ground and only dropped after a catastrophic failure of the crankshaft or suchlike. Interestingly, when I qualified as a Mechanic in 1978 and began a long career attempting to fix buses for a living it was immediately noticeable how many Bus Drivers did not drive their own cars.

This was a matter of simple economics...they could not afford to!

Buying, taxing, insuring and running a car was not then something which a Bus driver's wage had the Power to support except if supplemented by other means. As a shift mechanic one of *THE* most important calls one could get would be to attend to a broken down Ghost....Now there was a Code-Red if ever there was one.

One could be guaranteed that if that bus had failed, by the time the mechanic had got to it that every enthusiastic amateur employed by the board would have had a go at fixing whatever they perceived to be the problem.....which it rarely, if ever was!

Every little panel would have been opened, forcibly if necessary, relays shorted out, wires pulled off and joined together, usually in a shower of blue flashing sparks which would in turn blow every fuse not already blown and thereby rendering the thing a real breakdown.

Another noticeable aspect would be the sheer numbers of Staff on the Ghost.

Conductors who could not drive, Drivers who could not afford to own and run a car and a few Inspectors and Foremen who saw good sense in availing of a free service. Many would have even thrown an "all steel Raleigh" bicycle on as they were too knackered to pedal the uphill journey home after coasting downhill to work that morning or afternoon.

There would usually be a rousing cheer when you arrived followed by a mad rush to get onto the replacement bus you had driven out. If the batteries had gone flat, you had to be careful of keeping an eye on your "good" bus cos the Ghost driver might simply jump in and roar off leavin' you stuck on your Todd and having to send up a red flare for the Tow-Car...No Mobile Phones then either.

By and large the bus workforce tended to live in the Local Authority estates and saw nothing odd about it either.... relatively few were " purchasing" their houses and these were reckoned to be particularly savvy individuals who would be listened to with gravity if they deigned to give a few financial tips to the others.

Of course there were always the "Country Lads"...as yes... the boys who only came up for a summer job as a conductor and who never returned to their provincial roots,except in some tragic cases in a Pine Box.

These were times when we, the workers,knew our place and knew that life was always an uphill struggle with only a slim chance of beating its odds if you had a big win on the (illegal) Pools or the more Catholic (and legal) Prize Bonds.

Then if you were lucky you might even win a house in the annual Corporation Draw for those on the Housing List...now that was arriving in style! That lifestyle,in which so much was down to chance, now seems so old as to be Black and White or Sepia toned...and yet we know well that it was a vivid and enjoyable time too...with our working day taken up by all sorts of incredible noises and sensations as the products of Leyland Motors Limited disintegrated around us.

We did however prevail,ridding ourselves of those hugely individualistic machines,replacing them with another product which many considered theoretically impossible.....We manufactured something even *more* mechanically individual...The Bombardier Bus !

Now it could be argued that The Bombardier represented the beginning of an Era which saw the native Irish develop a sense of themselves as a Power on the World Stage with a vast array of hope that we could become a major exporter of things like this...sadly, apart from Baghdad we didn't manage to get a double-deck demonstrator into service on foreign soil...ah well..... there's always another day!

So perhaps as we nervously listen to the latest downward spiralling news about the Dow-Jones, The ISEQ, the DAX and heaven knows how many more Big Number indexes we need to step back a bit in time and recall a time when we really didn't have an arse in our trousers to use a Behanism which is as appropriate today as it was in his own era.

Oh yes ...times of plenty we have had,but times of scarcity did also come before.

THE MOTORIST

Ronnie Hickey

He holds the steering wheel
Firmly grasped
Between thumb, fingers and palm of hand,
Directing
This missile
At route and destination,
Responsible for those within
And those without.
Life and Death
Between thumb, fingers and palm of hand,
Daily and minute by minute.
Savouring
Exhilaration of journey
And joy of journeys end,
All held
Delicately balanced
Between thumb, fingers and palm of hand
By an ordinary man.

THE WHITE HOUSE

Joe Collins

About a quarter of a mile from where I grew up there as a large house within a walled garden. The house was always painted an off-white colour which gave it a spooky appearance. It was located toward the end of a country lane which was a cul-de-sac. It was just as well; nobody ever went near it as locals feared that it was haunted. On one side of the house there were ten windows two of which were blacked out and it was said that the rooms behind the blacked out windows were those that had been occupied by family members long deceased.

We did know that the family was made up of four adults, two sisters and two brothers all in their late 50s or early 60s and all unmarried. They were referred to locally as *The Quakers* but that meant nothing to me as a child.

Three members of the family were very quiet and retiring, however one of the brothers, the eldest deduced from his lead role in the Sunday morning march past drove a car, not very common at that time and even more uncommon was his membership of a flying club based at a small airport about 10 miles away. From time to time he flew his Cessna around the locality occasionally performing stunts such as rolling and tumbling and most scary of all climbing high and then steeply diving downward but pulling out of the dive at a safe distance from the ground as the onlookers screamed or covered their eyes for fear of the plane crashing to the ground.

The sisters were rarely seen in public except on a Sunday morning when the entire family walked past our house in single file and presumably in order of seniority on the way to the Meeting House with each one clutching what appeared to be a bible under the left arm, heads bowed, as monks in Mount Mellery, with not a word passing between them. The brothers never wore anything other than grey herring-bone tweed three piece suits, the sisters wore heavy ankle length skirts over which they wore tweed capes and on their heads, winter and summer, were knitted woollen bonnets. It amazed me that even on very wet Sundays they still walked despite the fact that they did have a car.

The non-flying brother rode on an old fashioned bicycle and he passed our house frequently. My father was an avid gardener and one day the cycling brother alighted from his bicycle and approached my father who was as always pottering around in the garden. The visitor said that he himself was a keen gardener and had, for years, as he cycled past our house admired my father's garden and his dedication to it throughout the four seasons.

They spoke for over half an hour and before he left he said that he would deliver some lily bulbs which my father could plant in time to flower the following spring.

The bulbs were planted and sure enough the following year we had a fantastic crop of lilies. At that time it was usual for girl Holy Communicants to carry a bunch of flowers on the special day. For many years every young girl in our area carried a bunch of lilies from our garden on her first Holy Communion day. It gave my father great pleasure when, on the Friday evenings before the first communion days, neighbours would come to our house and collect a bunch of lilies. No money changed hands but we received many photographs of the little angels dressed in their finery with the lilies draped over their arm.

About a year after the first engagement with my father the cycling brother stopped at our garden again. I was with my father at the time and the visitor said to my dad "send your son up to my house tomorrow afternoon and I will give him some eggs, honey and rhubarb". My father thanked him and said that I would go to the house at 3.00p.m. the next day if that suited, to which the man nodded in agreement.

On hearing this I was terrified. This house of mystery behind a high wall and large white gates which everybody feared I was now to visit. Not wanting to be labelled a 'Fraidy Cat'[a

Limerick expression] I set out on the following afternoon for the house.

On reaching the big gate I undid the latch and as the gate creaked open two large dogs came running down the driveway barking loudly. I turned quickly and ran back toward the closed gate. As I frantically tried to open it I heard a feeble female voice say "come in sonny the dogs won't touch you". I stopped for a moment to draw my breath and as I started to walk up the driveway the dogs came toward me again but they were much quieter now and plucking up courage I rubbed their heads which had a calming effect on them.

As I approached the front door of the house I looked to my left toward the garden and nearly fainted when I saw the figure of a human with what looked like a broad rimmed hat on the head with netting covering the face. I remembered seeing such a strange looking image in a Curly Wee annual being pushed along in a wicker wheelchair by, I think it was, the fox. My heart pounded and I turned to run toward the gate but the same feeble voice which I had heard earlier said "sonny come back, I am only wearing a beekeeper's hat with netting to protect me while I gather honey from the beehives".

I stopped again and went to the front door as directed by the voice from under the netting. I could not see a bell but there was a light rope by the side of the door. I pulled on it and there was a clanging noise that would awaken the dead. The tall sister opened the door and there before me appeared a large foyer with glass cases on three walls each filled with stuffed animals, birds and fish. There was a rabbit, a fox, a sheepdog, a few terriers, birds of prey, song birds and fish such as salmon, trout and larger ones whose names I did not know.

I was invited to follow the lady into the kitchen which was very large with presses reaching to the ceiling. These presses had many drawers with a label on each one denoting what it contained. There was a smell of bread baking in the Aga cooker which created a craving in me for a slice smothered with country butter. The lady sat me down and taking my basket she went into the room next door. She returned with the basket laden with rhubarb, tomatoes, leeks, a jar of honey, a jar of homemade jam and eggs in a cardboard tray resting on top of the other contents.

She must have sensed my longing for a slice of her oven-baked bread as she beckoned to me to sit at the table. And she produced a mug of milk and a large slice of her homemade bread on which she heaped butter scraped from what looked like a sandcastle one would make at the seaside. It was in fact a large block of homemade butter with a very salty taste.

While sitting there the other sister who had been collecting honey from the hives came in and up close she was even more frightening than earlier with her netted protective hat, gloves and a leather apron. As she removed this gear she explained that it was necessary to wear it when working at the hives. I had a fear of bees as I had been stung once which was very painful and caused my arm to swell up.

I thanked them for their kindness and as I left I was fearful that the dogs might run at me as I went toward the gate. However I was relieved when the tall sister said that she was taking the dogs for a walk in the field that went down to the stream at the end of their estate.

While I had mixed feelings about my visit to the mysterious house, the bread and butter tasted lovely I came away knowing that I never wanted to visit it again. When my father came home from work I told him that if there were any other plants, fruit or vegetables to be collected from the White House in the future he would have to go there himself. He laughed at me but after I had a few sleepless nights and nightmares on the nights that I managed some sleep he agreed that I would never be asked to go there again.

I did not go near the White House until about 25 years later when visiting my parents I walked up the country lane and to my horror I was confronted with a total wreck of a building, roofless, windows without glass swinging dangerously against what was left of a side wall and weeds growing to over ten feet in height. The walls which once surrounded the garden were no more than a heap of rubble. The entire sorry sight was a far cry from the house I had visited all those years ago. It brought to mind the following lines from Shelley's poem Ozymandias;

My name is Ozymandias king of kings
Look on my works ye mighty and despair
Nothing beside remains. Round the decay
Of that colossal wreck, boundless and bare
The lone and level sands stretch far away.

As I turned towards home I blessed myself with the sign of the cross and said a prayer for the repose of the souls of the four members of that Quaker family who over a quarter of a century earlier had been so kind to our family.

The difference for me was that in the intervening years I had become aware of the Society of Friends or as they were more commonly known The Quakers. The kindness which they displayed back then was in the true spirit of the Quaker ethos. After all they provided Food, Shelter, Clothing and Financial Assistance to our ancestors in famine times.